DEAD
TEASE

DEAD TEASE

A LOON LAKE MYSTERY

VICTORIA HOUSTON

TYRUS
BOOKS

a division of F+W Crime

Published by
TYRUS BOOKS
an imprint of F+W Media, Inc.
10151 Carver Road
Suite #200
Blue Ash, Ohio 45242
www.tyrusbooks.com

ISBN 10: 1-4405-3312-1 (Hardcover)
ISBN 13: 978-1-4405-3312-9 (Hardcover)
ISBN 10: 1-4405-3311-3 (Paperback)
ISBN 13: 978-1-4405-3311-2 (Paperback)
eISBN 10: 1-4405-3181-1
eISBN 13: 978-1-4405-3181-1

Printed in the United States of America.

10   9   8   7   6   5   4   3   2   1

Library of Congress Cataloging-in-Publication Data
is available from the publisher.

This is a work of fiction. Names, characters, corporations, institutions, organizations, events, or locales in this novel are either the product of the author's imagination or, if real, used fictitiously. The resemblance of any character to actual persons (living or dead) is entirely coincidental.

Many of the designations used by manufacturers and sellers to distinguish their product are claimed as trademarks. Where those designations appear in this book and F+W Media was aware of a trademark claim, the designations have been printed with initial capital letters.

This book is available at quantity discounts for bulk purchases.
For information, please call 1-800-289-0963.

Also Available in the Loon Lake Mystery Series:

For Melanie

"It's a shallow life that doesn't give a person a few scars."

~GARRISON KEILLOR

Chapter One

Buckling his belt as he leaned across his desk to peer out the office windows, Jim McNeil spotted Jen ambling her way to the hospital employee parking lot—a soft, satisfied expression on her face, which made him smile. As if she knew he would be watching, she came to an abrupt halt, turned toward the window, and flashed him a grin.

McNeil laughed, though he doubted she could see through the reflection of the early evening sun on the windows. But he knew she knew he was there. Fun. Boy, that girl is fun.

"Ah-h-h," he sighed as he straightened the pillows on the office divan and shoved the sheets into a blue plastic bin. Sliding the bin back into the coat closet, he set a stack of business magazines on top. He had learned a long time ago it was wise to keep the night janitors in the dark as to the bin's contents. Then he stepped into the bathroom.

When he accepted the CEO position at the small but prestigious Northwoods Medical Clinic, he hadn't counted on his office having a private bathroom, but what an indispensable perk it had become. Opening the medicine cabinet, he reached for a comb. Leaning into the mirror, he smoothed the shining waves of black into place, patted the graying sideburns, and with a slight smile examined his features.

You old devil, McNeil. He parted his lips and turned his head side to side checking his teeth. *How many times have you been told you look just like George Clooney? You devil, you.*

He wiped at a smudge of lipstick near his ear, grinned again, closed the cabinet, and checked his watch. He'd be home a half hour late but no big deal. Leigh never seemed to notice. Slipping his suit jacket off the hanger behind the closet door, he started down the hallway humming.

If only Leigh had a body as slender and tight as Jen's. But where Jen was lean and supple, Leigh was a pillow: wide and plump and so cushioned it was hard to get traction.

McNeil knew better than to complain. After all, his wife was easy to live with: eager to please, a darn good cook, and she took care of everything. At least she did until recently. The last few weeks it seemed something was up. Maybe her mother was sick. Or her silly worry that someone had been peeking in their windows.

"Oh, come on, kid, don't let your imagination run away with you," he had cautioned.

Shaking his head as he slid onto the front seat of the new forest green BMW convertible (he'd added a few of his own dollars to the allotment for a company car), McNeil reminded himself of the one sure way to go broke: divorce. Not on his agenda no matter how tight, cute, and fun. Been there, done that.

McNeil hit the buttons to raise the roof and snuggled into the driver's seat for a pleasurable drive home. The August heat hung heavy in the air as he coasted through the residential blocks of Loon Lake toward the highway.

Less than ten minutes later, he could feel the breezes off the lake as he neared their drive. Ah-h-h. Life is good.

Jen opened the sunroof on her Jeep Liberty and undid the top buttons on her shirt. Head back and eyes half closed, she waited for the light to change. God, the air feels great. She let her mind drift back over the afternoon.

Oh, man, guys like Jim McNeil are so easy to read. If she played this right, when he got bored and ready to try out the next new nurse, she would "understand" her way right up to running the department. No fool Jen Williams.

Still, she had to keep an eye out for crazy Cynthia down in ER. The bitch might have M.D. after her name but it ought to come with a C.N., too—"Certified Nuts." No sign of her today according to Jim. Not even a text on his phone. He better not take that for granted. She'd be back. Jen knew the type: they don't give up easy.

"I keep telling her I'm busy—think she gets the message?" Jim McNeil had asked Jen over drinks after the medical technology conference in Madison, where they had hooked up for the first time. He had admitted to a brief affair with Cynthia, whom he now found repellent.

"Doubt it. Better be prepared for her to call your wife."

"Oh? You think she'd go that far?"

Jen had shrugged. The woman was twice divorced and not even thirty-five yet, hardly the sign of a stable personality. And she was a bully who would not take being dumped easy. Jen's female colleagues at the clinic had been watching the developments between the CEO and the doc. They knew fireworks were brewing.

But Jen said nothing more about Cynthia. Romance is never kindled with negative remarks, and she had plans for McNeil. He might be a serial womanizer, but he was also a solid step on her way up.

At the top of the hill just before the turn into the condo parking lot, Jennifer spotted the old woman walking her little dog along the roadside. She could set her clock by that old lady, but maybe she walked that dog all day.

Walked her dog and, no matter how warm the day, she always wore purple: a purple trench coat with silver studs for buttons. Hopefully that would change when winter came. Purple is hard to see in the dark.

Jen drove down the slope and around the curve leading into the parking lot. On one side of the driveway was a grove of young balsam. On the other side was a bank of thirty mailboxes. Some guy she'd never seen before but pleasant-looking in jeans and a blue Oxford shirt was standing near the mailboxes and studying the names. He watched as she pulled her car into her parking spot, then walked over to check her mailbox.

"Can I help you?" she asked. He looked to be about her age, mid-twenties, and very tan under dark brown curly hair. Kinda cute. Maybe he was moving in? Jen smiled.

"Maybe. You Jennifer Williams?"

"How did you know?" She held out her right hand.

The knife slid cleanly, silently through her shirt and between her ribs. She slumped toward him—the open smile sagging into a soundless scream. He pushed her down and back under the hanging branches of balsam. He waited. No sound. He ran.

Chapter Two

As promised, the money was in an envelope under the driver's seat. He hadn't told her he would be borrowing the truck. But after he described it and where it would be parked, she assumed it was his. That was good. Even better—she followed through on her end of the deal.

Alvin tore open the envelope and counted, slapping the bills onto the ripped upholstery beside him. Wait. He counted again—only thirty bills? Fifteen hundred in fifties. Did that bitch short him five hundred bucks?

He peered into the envelope to be sure. Nope. No more bills. Okay, lady, you are asking for trouble. Big time. I don't do shit like this for nothin'. No sirree, no way, no how. He was so angry his heart pounded in his throat.

After cramming the money into his back pocket, Alvin tossed the envelope onto the floor and got out of the truck. Reaching for the knife that she had insisted he use, he walked to the back of the truck. It was a dandy knife, one he would like to keep, but he knew better than that. You don't watch *CSI* for nothin'.

Digging under a dirty tarp covering a heap of shingles in the bed of the rusted-out pickup, which he had borrowed from Jimbo, his buddy at the tavern where they did odd jobs, he found an oily rag and used it to give the knife handle a good wiping. Then, grasping the knife by the tip of the blade, he drew his right arm back and let fly. He watched as the knife sailed over the spindly aspens crowding the clearing.

Only then did he remember she had wanted him to return the damn thing. Oh well. They could discuss that when he stopped by for the rest of his money. If she wants it that bad, she can come out here and look for it herself.

Hey—that's right. Alvin pointed his index finger as if the woman was standing in front of him. He won't tell her where the knife is until she comes up with the cash. Yeah, that's the ticket.

The top branches of the aspens shook with a rustling sound and he turned to see a blur of neon reds, lime greens, and acid yellows coming at him. His heart stopped. It took a fraction of a second for his brain to register he was looking at two kids on mountain bikes barreling toward him. He jumped out of the way as they raced by hunched over their handlebars, legs pumping.

Shit! Had they seen him throw the knife? As fast as they had appeared, they were gone: a boy and a girl. Only now did he see evidence of bikes being used on this old dead end logging lane. The trail was barely visible but it was there. Damn. He should never have parked here. He'd have to hope . . .

Alvin stood still, his mind replaying the last few minutes. No, he was pretty sure they came riding through *after* the knife had landed. But he didn't like that they had seen him and the pickup parked out here. He struggled to remember their faces but they had flown by so fast, he'd caught only a glimpse. Oh well, he'd be long gone even if they did report him.

"Where's the knife?" she said, looking over his shoulder like she always did to be sure one of the old beaters he drove wasn't parked in her precious driveway.

"The knife is in a safe place and the truck is parked back behind that old barn down the road—just like you said."

He lied, but she wouldn't know. He'd left the truck right where it was parked while he took care of business. The walk to her house was less than a mile anyway. He needed that truck to get out of town. Jimbo wouldn't miss it 'til tomorrow for sure. Too late! He'd be in Michigan.

"Now where's the rest of my money? You told me two grand. I only got fifteen hunnert' in here," said Alvin, patting his back pocket. As he spoke, he felt his knees begin to tremble and his mouth go dry. He teetered as the ground shifted beneath him. He would need something soon.

"You don't look so good. You're so white—are you sick?" She motioned for him to follow her around to the back of the house.

"Not exactly."

Pausing as she reached the stone patio, she eyed him: could he be one of those meth creeps they say are everywhere these days? Probably just plain weird. Didn't matter either way, but she did need to get him off her property as soon as possible. While she wasn't expecting anyone, you never know in the Northwoods: people love to stop by.

"We agreed—two grand," he repeated, shoving his hands in his pockets to hide the trembling.

"Do I get the knife back?"

"When I get the money—" he said, grinding out the words.

"Okay. It's okay," she raised both hands to settle him down, "my mistake. I thought we had agreed on fifteen hundred but if I was wrong—"

"You bet your ass." Alvin wiped at the spittle on his chin.

"Al, you sit down, okay? Just relax. I'll be right back. I got cash in my purse."

He thought about following her and taking all her cash. Every penny. But he was too dizzy—his gums hurt and he was sure he had a fever—or maybe the day was hotter than he thought. Whatever. It was a relief to sink down on the wrought iron bench.

Stretching his right arm along the back of the bench, he closed his eyes, laid his head on his right shoulder, inhaled deeply, and waited. The distant hum of a motorboat made him drowsy. *Good idea: get paid, get stuff, take a nap.*

She opened the top drawer of the dining room buffet and reached under the linen place mats for the aluminum case Marv had hidden there for occasions like this. Well, kind of like this. He would be astonished to see her now.

She picked up the revolver. Nothing had changed since she had checked it last week: she could see it was fully loaded.

Funny. As she walked back toward the patio and the dumb shit waiting for her, it was amazing how every detail of the Women's Self-Defense training on the shooting range came back with absolute clarity. She snorted at the irony: she might have trouble locating her car keys thirty minutes from now but she sure as heck could remember how to use this handgun—and she took that class five years ago!

The memory of Marv had jogged another good thought: the freezer. He'd kept a bear in there once, and Alvin Marski was no black bear: he'd fit. She could figure out what to do about the freezer later. She paused at the sliding door to the patio. How to get the little creep *into* the freezer? She was strong but not that strong—and the last thing she needed was to put her back out.

Well then, she would just have to ask for help, wouldn't she. With that thought, she stepped through the doorway onto the patio. "Here, Alvin, exactly what I owe you. Please count it to be sure."

With a startled nod, Alvin took the bills and pushed himself up from the bench. A quick glance showed the money was there. He shoved the money into his back pocket and turned to leave.

"Oh, and Alvin," said the woman, "would you do one eensy-teensy favor for me before you leave? I have to move a box of frozen venison steaks from the freezer in the basement and it's so heavy. Do you mind just carrying the box up to the kitchen for me?"

"Okay," he said with a wheeze even though it was the last thing he wanted to do. "Where is it?"

Hoping he wouldn't trip—he was so dizzy—he followed her down the stairs to the workroom where a tall, wide upright freezer stood at one end. Walking over he yanked the door open. At first he thought the freezer was empty, but when he blinked and cleared his vision, all he saw was something wrapped in plastic on the only shelf, which was just above his head. "That it?"

"No, down there." Standing close behind him, the woman pointed to a cardboard box resting on the bottom and shoved to the back of the unit. Bending over, he leaned into the freezer to grab it.

Holding the gun in her right hand, left hand supporting her right wrist (exactly as she had been taught), she brought the revolver up and held it two inches behind his head. She pointed the muzzle at the base of his skull behind the left ear.

The first shot went in nicely but her instructor had said that small handguns don't kill, so she kept on firing until the double-action .22 Smith & Wesson 317LS revolver clicked on a spent round. She waited, breath held, but the target was not moving. She leaned over his shoulder, and checked for a pulse. Bleeding but not alive.

She checked his pockets. After slipping her money from his back pants pocket, she was able to push his torso farther into the open freezer. It helped that the kid wasn't huge. After some pushing and shoving, she managed to wrangle the box of venison off to one side, then out of the freezer. Now she could tuck the legs in, too. Very little blood had escaped the interior of the freezer, which made for a much easier cleanup than she had expected.

Less than fifteen feet away was the industrial double sink that Marv had installed years ago—a godsend she hadn't even counted on. After attaching the hose she used for cleaning her gardening tools, she was able to spray away the blood splatters on the floor and the outside of the freezer. She worked until the stream of water flowing down the floor drain was clear.

In less than thirty minutes she was ready to do one final check. Alvin was well situated in the freezer: curled up, head between his knees, he fit fine. She could see pools and splatters of blood inside the unit but nothing outside. She would check later to be sure there was no leakage. Otherwise: a clean job.

Surveying her handiwork, she spotted the carcass of a fox wrapped in plastic on the top shelf. She paused, then shrugged, closed the door, and fastened the padlock. *If no one has claimed that critter in the four years since it was set in there, they aren't likely to now.*

Up in the kitchen, she checked the time. Cocktail hour. Wonderful. She mixed a gin and tonic and strolled back out onto the patio. The stones had dried under the hot sun. Sitting in her favorite chair, she thought back over the afternoon and smiled to herself: she could not have done better planning ahead.

Of course, he must have left the knife in the truck, but that was parked behind an old abandoned barn. Forget it. Who would go looking there? And if they did, Alvin Marski was all over it anyway.

Gazing around her yard and along the wooden stairs leading down to the lake, she remembered the tree man: George. Not only was he cheap when it came to cutting trees but twice now he had been happy to cart away worn-out appliances and dispose of them in such a way that she had been able to avoid outrageous landfill fees.

Of course! She sipped her drink.

He had charged her ten bucks to dump the old Maytag washer. This might be worth an extra five, though—that freezer is heavy. And if she told him she'd lost the key to the padlock on the door, he wouldn't care. Plus he's too dumb to notice. But she better make it twenty just to keep him happy.

Ah, yes, she sipped again. It was nearly eight o'clock and the sun was dipping below the pines but the night was warm. August warm.

Only one obstacle remained: that fat wife.

The ice in her drink clinked as she raised the glass to toast herself. Her eyes, fierce as an eagle's, glittered in the fading light.

Chapter Three

"Doc, if you will hold this sucker steady here, I'll pull the cord over and around and try not to lose an eye doing it. . . ."

On his knees in the sand beside the dock, Paul Osborne's neighbor struggled to rig a bright yellow fiberglass kayak with a long black bungee cord tipped with a red metal hook that appeared capable of springing loose and taking critical body parts with it.

Osborne kept his own head down and out of the way. Years of practicing dentistry in the Northwoods where hockey pucks claimed more teeth than Easter candy had taught him to avoid airborne inanimate objects, particularly those with a projectile punch.

He considered offering a word of caution, but he knew from experience that once the man in the faded blue sweatshirt stenciled "Romance, Excitement, and Live Bait: You Can Have It All at Ray's Place" set his heart on a new money-making venture, there was no getting in his way. Not even when said venture might be life threatening.

"I don't understand why you need such a long bungee," said Osborne, doing his best to keep the kayak from slipping sideways.

"So I can carry my goddamn fishing rods on the side," said Ray Pradt between clenched teeth. "Why the hell do you think?"

"Well," said Osborne, opting to risk a reasonable commentary even though he knew better, "I'm looking at a thirty-thousand-dollar bass boat moored ten feet from here. The dock where it's tied up appears to be anchored to land that belongs to you. Given that bass boats were designed to carry all sorts of fishing gear, I'm perplexed. Correct me if I'm wrong but aren't kayaks for Type A's who don't have the patience to fish?"

Ray didn't answer as he leaned forward, one arm extended to maintain tension in the bungee cord while he scrambled with the other to hook the cord somewhere inside the fiberglass craft.

Watching Ray while holding the kayak steady, Osborne was reminded of an origami heron that one of his granddaughters had folded for a school art class. With elbows and knees pointing in all directions, his six feet five inches folded into multiple sections and his long arms capable of a giant wingspread, Ray Pradt lacked only the serenity of a Great Blue Heron.

The cord caught and held. Both men gave a sigh of relief, and Ray, leaning back, wiped the sweat from his forehead. He brushed back the mass of dark brown curls that had fallen into his eyes—an effort that gave him the appearance of having had prolonged exposure to a light socket.

"You okay if I let go now?" asked Osborne, feeling a cramp in his right hamstring.

"Yep. This'll work," said Ray. "Check it out, Doc." He got to his feet, pointed to the kayak with pride, and waved his right hand in a mock brushstroke saying, "All that's left is for me to paint 'Ride the Muskie' on each side and she's ready. Yep, this . . . is . . . sweet."

"Sweet? *Sweet?*" Osborne shook his head, befuddled. "That is one weird contraption. Nothing *sweet* about it."

"Doc, you need to get out more. Trust me," said Ray, shaking an authoritative finger as he spoke, "kayak fishing is the new sport fisherman's dream—huge on the East Coast where they compete to see who can catch the biggest blue fin tuna."

"Tuna," said Osborne. "When was the last time you saw tuna in Loon Lake?"

Ignoring the remark, Ray launched into a routine too familiar to Osborne, who surrendered to being held hostage as his neighbor sat back on his heels and—with words and pauses stretched out like chewing gum—rambled on happily: "Just you imagine, Doc . . . sitting . . . right? Just sitting . . . in this little humdinger here . . . with the water *this* close. . . ."

He measured two inches between his thumb and forefinger to demonstrate how deep a kayaker sits in the water, "When you get a strike . . . and Wham! You got a muskie on the line and . . . *and* . . . that fish is huge enough to pull you right along at . . . maybe," the eyebrows raised high in anticipation, ". . . fifteen miles an hour.

"Think of that, Doc." Ray leaned toward Osborne, his eyes sparkling, "You might be fighting . . . nose to nose. Hell, now that I think of it—I might have to get this kayak a *powerboat* registration." Ray grinned at his own joke.

"And?" said Osborne, waiting.

"And what?"

"How do you get the fish home? You sure as heck can't boat it."

"Yeah," the grin faded, "I gotta think about that."

"And you expect people to pay for this? When they can sit in comfort on a bass boat with a six-pack at their feet?"

"Like I said—kayak fishing is huge on the East Coast. Doc," said Ray, sounding eager to change the subject, "I want you and Lew to try one of these fly fishing. Rig up some good-size streamers—see if you can catch a muskie on a dry fly. Lew will love it, I know she will."

With a shake of his head, Osborne walked onto the dock and out toward the bench on the end where he often sat with his friend to relish the final moments of the setting sun. Sitting down, he paused to look back and say, "How did you happen to get into all this? Don't you have your hands full guiding clients?"

"I made a deal with a marina up in Bayfield when I was fishing Lake Superior last week. They'll cut me in for thirty percent on every fishing kayak I sell."

"I see," said Osborne, deciding not to ask any more questions. If Ray followed his usual pattern, this crazy idea would fade fast. "Got time for a ginger ale?"

"Yep, some in the cooler on the boat there, Doc. You sit tight, I'll grab us a couple."

Osborne gazed across the lake toward the far shoreline where the sun ripped a scarlet tear in the sky above the spires of distant pines. "What a night," he said, popping the tab off the can Ray handed him. "No wind, eighty degrees. A perfect August evening."

"Maybe in your world," said Ray, sitting down beside him, "but I had two guiding jobs canceled thanks to this hot weather."

"Sorry to hear that," said Osborne. He was feeling fine: satisfied, relaxed, looking forward to a late dinner, maybe even staying over at Lewellyn's. Was it fair for him to be so happy?

Just as he was mulling over his state of contentment, his cell phone rang. He reached into the chest pocket of his khaki shirt. "Oops, excuse me a minute—it's Lew, I better take it."

"Hello?"

"Doc, where are you?"

"Ray's. Helping him do some damage to a kayak. What's up?"

"Gotta cancel dinner and I need you. Stabbing victim out at the new condos back behind the clinic. Can't use Pecore on this one—the victim is his niece.

"Good thing you're at Ray's 'cause, Doc, if he's got the time—I sure would appreciate it if he would shoot the crime scene tonight. With this hot weather and chance of a thunderstorm, I don't dare wait for the Wausau boys to get here in the morning. Even if we move the victim tonight, I don't have to tell you what can happen to my trace evidence—"

"Pecore's niece? You don't mean Jen Williams?" Osborne caught Ray's eye as he spoke.

"Yes. Meet me there ASAP. Both of you, please. The victim is under the trees across the road from the mailboxes—right at the parking lot. You can't miss it."

"What's up with Jen?" said Ray after Osborne had clicked off his phone. "We dated a few years back. She's a little scary."

"Not any more," said Osborne.

Chapter Four

"A clean wound, Lew, with no bruising or abrasion that I can see," said Osborne, keeping his voice low as he spoke to Lewellyn Ferris, the Loon Lake chief of police who was kneeling beside him, taking notes as he worked. A sterile tarp designed to keep debris or footprints from contaminating the area around the victim had been put in place before Osborne arrived.

Hands encased in nitrile gloves, he had unbuttoned the young woman's shirt—so dark with blood he couldn't tell it was light blue until he tugged it up from where it was belted at her waist—then gently pushed aside the edge of the blood-soaked bra covering her left breast. After examining the wound, he dabbed at the blood surrounding the site where the knife had entered, waited, and dabbed again. "Lew, I want to be sure we have only one . . ." He didn't finish his sentence.

It was less than an hour since the 911 call had come in from the condo resident who had walked up to get his mail only to be confronted by the sight of Jennifer Williams's body shoved under the low branches of the balsam firs.

Osborne's fingers prodded the perimeters of both breasts, then across the rib cage, making sure. When he was certain, he straightened up and whispered so only the woman at his side could hear: "The cause of death appears to be a stab wound produced by a sharp object and resulting in a wound deeper than wide . . . ," he paused. "Enough for now?" It was his responsibility to complete the death certificate but he knew it could be amended after the autopsy.

Lewellyn Ferris nodded. She saw what he saw, and they both knew without having to be told by the boys from the Wausau Crime Lab that the knife had penetrated the heart—death had been instantaneous.

A murmur of excitement from a cluster of bystanders huddled across the road escalated as the van from Channel 12-TV pulled up less than ten feet from the row of mailboxes behind which lay the body. Scrambling to her feet and taking care not to disturb the sterile tarp beneath her, Lew strode toward the van with both hands up to silence the young female reporter thrusting a microphone at her: "No comment until we have notified the family. I want everyone back, way back—and stay there."

When she was satisfied she had been obeyed, Lew returned to where Osborne was busy entering the results of his exam on the clipboard propped against his long, black medical examiner's bag. He looked up as she approached, and both glanced back at the body. He'd left Jen's shirt open for the crime scene photos.

"That blade had to be so sharp—see where it went through the cloth and a section of that bra without tearing?" Osborne gestured with his pen. "Not even a loose thread. How many people have knives that sharp? Hunters maybe."

"Only in deer season, Doc."

Osborne got to his feet, zipped shut the black bag and, picking it up, backed away with slow, careful steps. "For no good reason—except for how sharp the knife had to be—I don't think this was a spontaneous act."

Lew shrugged. "Hard to say, really. Could be a robbery gone bad? But I appreciate your intuition, Doc. Won't hurt to put that in your notes."

Looking up, she studied the sky overhead. "The good news is the switchboard called to tell me the weather forecast has changed: a slight chance of rain tonight with light winds. But good cover from these pines, which will make it easier to recover any trace evidence.

I'll have Todd cordon off this side of the driveway from the turn-off into the condo complex up to the first building and leave it for the Wausau Crime Lab to work up in the morning."

"You talked to them? What did they say?" asked Osborne, wondering if he needed to wait at the morgue for one of the Wausau boys to arrive.

"Not yet, Doc. I'll give 'em a call in a few minutes but I doubt I can get anyone up here tonight. Ridiculous to work an outdoor crime scene in the dark." She gave a sigh of reluctance, reminding Osborne how much fun she had dealing with the bozo running the crime lab.

The director of the Wausau Crime Lab made it his mission to give the Loon Lake chief of police a hard time. If he wasn't trying to share an off-color joke—with females as a punch line—he enjoyed ranting about women in law enforcement: "Ladies do not belong in military combat or on the police force—they are too soft." Lew would listen until she got what she wanted.

As far as Osborne was concerned, that razzbonya got one thing real wrong: *soft* did not apply to Lewellyn Ferris.

"Try your buddy Bruce this time," said Osborne. "Skip his boss and throw in fly fishing for muskies—from a kayak. Bet you anything he'll jump at that."

"*What* are you talking about? Are you teasing me?" Lew grinned, a friendly challenge in her eyes. Osborne smiled back. He found her so cute when she did that—but he knew better than to say so. Nevertheless, he allowed himself a moment to feel sixteen again.

"I'll tell you later. Ray's latest enterprise."

"Oh no," still smiling, Lew rolled her eyes. "But speak of the devil. If you're finished, I'll have Ray get the photos now."

She waved a go-ahead to Ray who had been chatting with several of the men and women gathered across the road. In one hand he held a tripod and in the other a camera he used on more pleasant occasions: shooting outdoor vistas for the annual Lions Club calendar. He walked over to where Lew and Osborne were standing.

"Ready for me to take over, Chief?" asked Ray.

"Yep, you know the drill. But shoot the victim first, I don't want her exposed like that any longer than necessary."

"Of course. I'll do that right away so the EMTs can move her—then the site. If it gets too dark, I have extra spotlights in the truck."

"You sure you're okay with this?" Lew asked. "Doc mentioned Jen Williams was a friend of yours—"

"Not really," said Ray, his eyes serious and sad. "We dated a few times maybe five years ago. That's all. She used me for sport."

Lew gave him a questioning look. "We'll discuss that later."

A silver-gray Ford Taurus pulled up behind Lew's police cruiser. The passenger's side door was already open and a short, stout woman in gray Bermuda shorts and an oversized white T-shirt with bright orange squirrels across the front jumped from the car, leaving the door open behind her. Moving surprisingly fast for a woman built so low and wide, she dashed to where Ray was setting up near the body, slipping and nearly falling in a rivulet of blood that had escaped into a groove along the driveway.

As she closed in on the white tarp covering the site where the body lay, Lew stepped forward to block her way. "Stop, please, you can't go there," she said, grabbing the woman by her left arm.

"I'm her mother for God's sake. I'm here to help—" The woman yanked her arm away but at the sight of her daughter sprawled on the ground she stopped. Her hands flew to her mouth as she cried, "Oh my God. Oh my God, but they just called me! She's already—? No. No. No. Can't be. Not my Jen. The person who called—" the woman whirled around as if she could find the guilty caller in the crowd across the road.

Osborne looked down and away from the helplessness. He knew that pain. At least this time it wasn't his. He waited, wishing as he had learned to do: if only someone could turn back the clock—just one hour—to give this poor woman the chance to maybe call her daughter and ask her to come by Mom's house instead of going straight home to her apartment? If only . . .

"You've made a mistake! I know you did! Let me see," the woman struggled to get past Lew. "That's not Jennifer. She never wears red. Oh . . . oh . . ."

Osborne hurried over. "Bonnie," he said to the woman who had been a patient of his for years before his retirement, "Chief Ferris and I—we know that the victim is your daughter . . . Jennifer. And I am so sorry but . . . well . . . we need you to officially identify the body." It was an outrageous request, and he hated hearing himself make it.

The woman's breath kept catching as she tried to talk. "Is she—is she? When did this happen?"

"Shortly after six we think," said Lew. "One of my officers checked the clinic, so we know Jennifer left the building at six or a little after. The call came in right at six thirty."

"Oh God," the woman dropped her head. She slumped to one side, and Osborne caught her shoulders before she collapsed. Together he and Lew eased her back along the road and onto the passenger seat of Lew's squad car where she sat motionless, staring at the floor of the car. Her breath was coming in short bursts but she was not crying, not saying anything. Osborne hoped to hell she wasn't having a heart attack.

"Chief Ferris, I . . . want . . . to . . . see . . . my . . . child."

"Okay," said Lew, "Dr. Osborne and I will help you over there but I have to show you right where to walk so we don't compromise any trace evidence that may have been left by the killer."

"A killer? She was murdered?" Bonnie Williams looked up at them, amazement on her face. "I thought she was hit by a car. You're telling me she was *murdered*?"

Chapter Five

As Bonnie approached, Ray moved his tripod to one side and stepped back to let her kneel on the tarp. Leaning forward, she reached out to stroke the inside of her daughter's bare wrist where it rested on a cushion of pine needles. Then, bending over Jen's face, she murmured soft words as she kissed the pale forehead. Placing the back of her right hand to each temple, she seemed to be checking to be sure there was no hint of warmth.

Osborne watched the woman's hands moving over the still form. Love, not death, infused these final moments with her child. He glanced over at Lew whose eyes were focused on a distant place: a place known only to a parent who has also lost a child.

As the older woman pressed her hands against the ground to push herself up, Osborne took her by the elbow. "Bonnie," he said as she got to her feet and grabbed his arm to steady herself, "Bonita, come here." He opened his arms and the woman walked into them, burrowing her wet face into his shirt as deep sobs shook her frame. He held her close.

Looking over at Lew, he said, "Bonnie and her late husband were patients of mine, Chief Ferris. Jennifer, too, when she was still in high school." Lew nodded.

Jen had been a genetic mirror of her father: she had his height and lean build, his light Scandinavian coloring with white-blond hair and angular cheekbones. Only locals familiar with the family would have guessed she was also the daughter of the short, full-bodied woman with black eyes, salt-and-pepper hair, and wide, generous smile whose grandparents had emigrated from Poland during the Northwoods' logging heyday of the 1880s.

Since his retirement three years ago, Osborne had known Jen by reputation only. More than once the McDonald's crowd had relished tales of her spirited bad behavior—summer pontoon parties featuring too much booze and skinny-dipping being a frequent highlight. On the other hand, like many people in Loon Lake, he was more familiar with her mother's upbeat nature and reliable good humor.

Though Bonnie had been widowed by a mill accident twenty years ago and, since then, put in long hours at the Customer Service desk in the Loon Lake Market, she always had a smile for customers. And a happy update on her "crazy" daughter—Jen's graduate degree in graphic arts, her return to Loon Lake for a "terrific" job at the clinic, the new KitchenAid mixer she had given her mom for her birthday.

Osborne tucked his head down over Bonnie's. Why? Why did this kind, hardworking woman have to lose that one wild and precious child of hers?

"If it helps," he said in a soft tone when he felt the tears subside every so slightly, "Jennifer died instantly. No pain. I doubt she even knew what was happening."

"I hope you're right." Bonnie tipped her head back to peer up at him. Lew handed her a bunch of Kleenex. As she wiped at her face she said, "But, Dr. Osborne, how would you know? You're a dentist—" She turned to Lew, "Where's my brother-in-law? Shouldn't Herb be here?"

Bonnie Williams was the middle child of three siblings. A younger sister, Sylvia, was married to the mayor of Loon Lake and an older sister, Donna, was married to Herb Pecore, the Loon Lake coroner whose job was a political appointment and a headache for the Loon Lake chief of police.

Among Pecore's qualifications for the position were bankrupting a beer bar (hard to do in the Northwoods) and training Black and Tan Coonhounds to tree bears. Other virtues included chronic alcoholism, peripatetic office habits, and gross incompetence when it came to the chain of custody on criminal evidence. Once he had even managed to misplace the physical evidence from a murder case.

Not that any of that made a difference. Nor did curses, eye-rolling, and written complaints from Chief Lewellyn Ferris. Pecore's job was well protected thanks to his (and Bonnie's) brother-in-law, the mayor. When Chief Ferris found herself pushed to the limit, she maintained her sanity by going fishing. Or moonlighting as a fly fishing instructor for the local sporting goods store. Either way, she could escape the distress of working with a fool.

And so it was that after giving a private lesson to the recently retired dentist, Dr. Paul Osborne, Officer Lewellyn Ferris (not yet promoted to "chief") had been thrilled to find she had not only an interesting new student but a connection with someone skilled in forensic dentistry who could be deputized to help the Loon Lake Police identify victims and establish cause of death on those occasions when Pecore was "incapacitated."

For Osborne his first evening in a trout stream was an equally auspicious encounter. Who knew that signing up for a lesson in fly fishing—for the sole purpose of helping him decide if he should or shouldn't sell an expensive fly rod he had purchased years ago but never used—might change his life?

At first, he had been taken aback when the fly fishing instructor he was to meet at the parking lot—a "Lou" recommended and booked for the evening by Ralph's Sporting Goods—turned out to be "Lew," a woman he recognized from her younger days as a parent when she brought her children in for their annual school dental exams.

Things had changed since then. Her son and daughter had grown up, she'd left her job as a secretary at the mill and, after a divorce, earned a degree in law enforcement after which she joined the Loon Lake Police Department.

Osborne, meanwhile, had raised two daughters, lost a wife, and given up a profession he dearly loved due to the badgering of the late wife who had insisted they "travel, put more money into redecorating our house instead of all that ridiculous fishing equipment, and spend time entertaining—Paul, you know how I love dinner parties. . . ."

And so it was that though they may have been aware of one another for years, it wasn't until they were standing hip deep in the riffles of the Prairie River on a moonlit summer night that they discovered they just might *need* each other.

"Because your brother-in-law is so closely related to the victim, I'm afraid we can't have him handle this part of the investigation, Bonnie," said Lew. "But please don't worry. For two years now, Doctor Osborne has worked for the department on an 'as-needed' basis. He is deputized to assist the Loon Lake Police as deputy coroner when Herb isn't available. Be assured, the Wausau Crime Lab will handle the crime scene investigation."

Bonnie may or may not have understood, but she nodded as if she did. From where she had been waiting near the Ford Taurus, another woman, less chunky than Bonnie but similar in coloring, approached them.

"Chief Ferris," said Sylvia Tillman, the mayor's wife, "I'm here for my sister. Can she come with me now or . . . ?"

"Hello, Sylvia," said Lew. "A few more minutes, please. If Bonnie can manage, I have several questions critical to our investigation. Do you mind waiting?"

"No, of course not," said Sylvia. She rubbed her sister's shoulder then walked back to wait by her car.

"Bonnie," said Lew, steering her by the elbow to the passenger side of the squad car, "why don't you sit here. . . ." She opened the car door and helped Bonnie slide onto the front seat. "I'll close the door and run the air conditioning. It'll be comfortable and give us some privacy. Dr. Osborne will join us. Based on what he found during his exam, he may have a few questions for you as well."

Bonnie pointed at the ambulance crew who were waiting for a signal from Lew to move the body. "They'll be careful with Jen, right?"

"Please don't worry. They know what to do. I can arrange for you to visit her in the hospital morgue once she's there."

"Okay," said Bonnie, tears glimmering at the sound of the word "morgue."

Before walking around the front of the cruiser to the driver's side, Lew motioned for Osborne to meet with her behind the squad car. In a low voice she said, "Don't hesitate to jump in, Doc. I can see you know Bonnie better than I do."

Osborne nodded and slipped into the back seat.

Early on, he and Lew had discovered they made a good team when it came to interrogating people. Whether it was gender differences or their varied experiences over the years of life in Loon Lake, each was capable of hearing the same words from the same person in different ways. Comparing notes later, they were often surprised at what the other had heard—or missed—or had a different interpretation of the same answer.

Osborne's years of listening between the lines to better diagnose patients' problems offered a counterbalance to Lew's targeted questions, which, on more than one occasion, had led to an argument. Given the grim circumstances, Osborne was more than a little chagrined to admit he enjoyed these sometimes-heated exchanges. Loved how her eyes flashed when she was challenged.

"Bonnie, this is not to make any assumptions whatsoever but can you tell us who Jennifer has been dating?" Lew asked.

"No one that I know of. Not recently anyway." Bonnie blew her nose and settled back against the car seat.

"Really?" Surprise flashed across Lew's face. "How old was she?"

"Twenty-six."

"Old boyfriends? A partner, maybe? She's young but had she ever been married and divorced?"

"Jenny dated Bart Martin when she first moved back, but that's been over for a long time. He married Candy Phelan last Christmas—but he and Jen have stayed friendly. *Were* friendly." Tears shimmered again.

"How long has she been living in the condos here?"

"She moved in right when they opened six months ago." Bonnie took a deep breath and exhaled. "She loved this place . . . she has the nicest condo unit. . . ." Lew tapped a pen on her notepad, thinking, then said, "Has she been upset with anyone lately? A neighbor? A friend? Anyone she worked with?"

"Umm, not really. Once in a while she talked about work stuff but that was more frustration not anger."

"Doc?" Lew turned toward Osborne in the back seat.

"Has she mentioned if anyone has been bothering her?" said Osborne. "Anyone ask her out who might have made her feel uncomfortable? Obscene phone calls? E-mails or other intrusive behavior from people?"

Bonnie shook her head. "No . . . not that I'm aware of. When it comes to dating or people asking her out, we . . . well, I never asked about her relationships with men. We've never been the kind of mother-daughter to share every little thing. . . . I suppose that's my fault—I should know more."

"Heavens, no," said Lew, "I understand. My daughter and I are the same. We keep our private lives off-limits, but maybe she would have a girl friend who might know?"

"Her closest friend is Kerry Schultz who works at the clinic, too. She's a surgical nurse. I can get you her home phone number if that would help. I have it at home."

"Yes, please," said Lew. "Here's my card with my cell phone number. Call me with that as soon as you can—or anything else you may think of. Anytime. I don't mind."

"What about the patients and staff at the hospital?" said Osborne. "Anyone there with whom she might have had some difficulty?"

"Well, she sure as heck doesn't care for that goofy surgeon they got working the emergency room," said Bonnie, her voice rising. "That's the only person she had any problems with that I'm aware of. But, I think all the gals at the clinic have problems with her."

"What kind of problems?" Lew gave her a sharp look.

"The usual—she's bossy, blames the nurses for her mistakes. Brownnoses the bigwigs. The nurses all hate her. You can ask Kerry—she'll tell you." Bonnie lowered her voice as if sharing a confidence: "You should see the way she dresses . . . the cleavage. . . . Well, Jen had no use for her, I tell you."

Ten minutes later, after walking Bonnie over to her sister's car, Osborne joined Lew in the front seat of the cruiser. "Hold on, Doc," she said, radio mike in her hand, "I'm being patched through to Harold at the crime lab." She winked and waited.

The head of the Wausau Crime Lab answered right away.

"Wausau Crime Lab, Harold Eckes speaking."

"Lew Ferris, Harold. How're you doing?"

"Oh, you. What do you want now?" He sounded as if all Lew did was call and make his life difficult.

"Sorry to bother you so late in the day, Harold," said Lew, keeping her voice deliberately upbeat, which she knew was guaranteed to drive him nuts. She described what had happened and her efforts to protect the crime scene.

"You got the budget for this?"

"We'll find the money. We have to, don't we," said Lew. "I will have the victim transported down to Wausau first thing in the morning. I was hoping maybe your man, Bruce Peters, might be available?"

"Don't know. Call him yourself."

Harold was off the line before Lew could mention she wouldn't need Bruce's cell phone number. She grinned at Osborne. "Mission accomplished."

Osborne patted her on the shoulder. "Good work, Lewellyn. Harold thinks he's making your life miserable and you got what you wanted."

"I enjoy torturing the guy," said Lew. "Doesn't speak well of me but—"

"If it's okay with you," said Osborne as he opened the car door and moved to leave, "I will accompany the ambulance down to the morgue and finish my paperwork there. Too tired for my place tonight?"

"I don't know. What do you have in the fridge?"

"Leigh, I like how you've set up the TV and the bar out here on the deck," said Jim McNeil as he settled into a wicker armchair and swung his feet up onto a matching ottoman.

"Oh, honey, I thought you would," said Leigh, sitting down across from him and picking up the afghan she was crocheting. "I thought this way we can relax together. You can watch the news, a little baseball—and enjoy the cool night air while I do my needle-work. I get so tired of the air conditioning. Did you have a good day?"

She let her eyes rest on her handsome husband. He had changed into the green golf shorts and white polo shirt with a matching LaCoste crocodile that she had given him for his birthday.

"Who cares how the day went. Right now I got the remote in one hand and a G&T in the other, kiddo. Life is good." He smiled at her then looked back at the screen.

"I thought you might enjoy this, sweetie," said Leigh McNeil, hoping he would call her something other than "kiddo" one of these days. How long had it been since he had told her he loved her? Years? As always, she pushed that thought away.

Ice cubes clinking in their drinks, they were watching Channel 12's evening broadcast when a reporter broke into the sports news: "This just in from the Loon Lake Police. The victim of a late afternoon stabbing at the new Lake Thompson Shores condos has been identified as Jennifer Williams, a twenty-six-year-old Loon Lake resident. . . ."

"Jim, sweetie," said Leigh, "Jennifer Williams. Doesn't she work at your clinic?"

Chapter Six

The lake was tranquil, an amethyst basin studded with millions of stars. Osborne, legs extended with his ankles crossed, relaxed on the wooden bench at the end of his dock as he sipped from a glass of iced tea. It seemed the perfect choice for a nightcap to accompany the soft slurps of feeding fish while he waited to hear the grind of Lew's tires in the driveway.

He smiled as peals of laughter and murmuring voices drifted his way from the far shore. They sounded so close they might have come from the cabin next door. Muted applause from a bonfire glowing at the south end of the lake testified to a late night for young campers. Overhead, bats swooped, threading their way through the branches of the hovering white pine.

Osborne savored the warm air, acknowledged his good fortune, and sipped again. The night was charmed—except for random thoughts of poor Jennifer Williams whom he had left tucked under a cold coverlet in the hospital morgue.

Before leaving the morgue he had arranged for an early morning transport to the Wausau Crime Lab for an autopsy. *Oh, Jennifer*, he thought, *so young, too young. So full of life less than twelve hours ago and now . . .* Osborne slapped at a mosquito missed by the bats.

A Harry Belafonte tune shrilled from his cell phone, shattering the peace like the shriek of a rabbit losing its head to a great horned owl. He answered.

"Dad? Sorry to call so late. Do you have a minute?"

"Erin—is everyone okay?" He sat straight up on the bench. Osborne dreaded late night phone calls: death, dismemberment in a car crash or a hockey puck in the mouth—good news never arrived late. And hockey pucks were the least of his worries.

"We're fine, we're fine, but—" He could hear the tension in his youngest daughter's voice and held his breath over what she might say next.

"Honey, what is it?"

"Well, Dad, I hate to ask you this but, well, we have a problem with Beth. Mark and I have been planning all summer to take the kids to Chicago tomorrow to visit museums and Beth is refusing to go. She has basketball camp every day this week and insists she can't play varsity if she misses a day. Could she—gosh, I hate to ask you this—but is there any chance she could stay with you?"

"You mean out here at my place? Sure, why not? Of course, she'll have to do the cooking—just kidding. I'd love to have her." He relaxed back on the bench.

"You don't have to drive her to camp—she can bike in from the lake and . . ." Erin laid out the details of his eldest granddaughter's schedule.

"Now, don't worry," said Osborne when she was finished. "Beth and I will have a good time together. What the heck—maybe Lew and I'll take her fishing."

"Oh, golly, Dad, I love you. I'll drop her stuff off at your place in the morning and I'll have the schedule written down. Oh, one more thing, Dad. She's not allowed to text more than fifteen times a day."

"What? How do you regulate that?" Osborne was puzzled.

"I'll show you in the morning. There's an 800 number where you can check on it. It's easy."

Pausing on the stone stairs leading down to Osborne's dock, Lew let her eyes adjust to the darkness. No lanterns lit the way this evening, which surprised her, but the reflection on the water from the stars overhead made it easy to spot Osborne at the far end of the dock. He was leaning forward, elbows on his knees, a cell phone held tight to one ear. No wonder he hadn't heard her drive up.

She watched him talking. Moonlight outlined the sturdy contours of his face: a face that had a way of lightening her heart. He was a very good-looking man, and she liked that he was not aware of that. Or if he was, it was an awareness that had come late in life—late enough that he was not one of those jerks who are so good-looking that they never make the effort to be interesting.

That was not Paul Osborne. Not only did he never cease to intrigue her but he had a knack for making her feel like she was the most fascinating person he knew. And that she did not mind. Nice to feel appreciated. Maybe treasured? Whatever. Just watching him talk on his cell phone eased the tensions of the day.

"Oh, Lew," said Osborne, clicking his phone off as she strolled onto the dock, "sorry—I didn't hear you drive up or I would have turned on the lights." He reached toward a tall plastic glass and a pitcher sitting on a small table beside the bench. "A glass of iced tea sound good?"

"Certainly does," she said in a determined tone as she slid onto the bench beside him. He laid his arm across her shoulders, and she snuggled into the curve of his long, lean frame. "What a day, Doc. What a sad day."

"Any new developments since I left for the morgue?"

"Not much to work with. The only person anyone appears to have seen in the vicinity before Jennifer was attacked was an elderly woman walking her dog. Apparently she walks the dog every day near the condos. I'm hoping to question her tomorrow. She may have seen something.

"Oh, and a woman whose unit is next door to Jennifer's said she thought she saw someone peeking in Jennifer's windows last Saturday night, but it was late and she didn't get a good look at the person. Couldn't say if it was male or female. Problem is the sidewalk runs right along there so it could have been a perfectly innocent individual walking by at a time when Jennifer had her curtains open and they happened to look in. You know, like we all do when we're night fishing and we go by a place all lit up.

"So, Doc, who was that you were talking to? No one looking for me, I hope."

"That was Erin—Beth will be staying with me for a few days. She's refusing to go with the family to Chicago. Basketball camp."

"Hmm," said Lew, tipping her head up with a teasing grin on her face. "Really? Basketball camp instead of a trip to the big city? And she's fourteen, right? Sounds like a boy to me."

"Erin didn't say anything about boys."

"Check with her. I've raised a daughter. Fourteen is a challenging age."

"Lewellyn, is this a good thing or a bad thing we're talking about here?"

Lew snorted. "It's a human thing, Doc." She gave him an affectionate poke with her elbow. "Speaking of humans, if you have the time, I can really use your help tomorrow. I want to talk with everyone who has been working with Jen Williams at the clinic. And as many friends as we can locate—men, women. Maybe she was in a pool league, played softball.

"Meanwhile, I've arranged to have Todd and Dani question the residents at the condos and nearby neighbors—except that old lady with the dog. She's on my list."

"Dani is so new to the force," said Osborne. "Are you sure she can handle interrogations like this?"

"She and Todd will work as a team. And there is no one better than Dani on the computer when it comes to background checks. That girl can find where you buy your dog food!

"No, I'm not worried, Doc. When it comes to people—and it may be thanks to her training as a hairdresser—but that girl has excellent intuition. She sure got a read on Pecore right away." Lew chuckled. "Who knew cosmetology prepared you for police work?"

Lew had met Dani when she was a student of cosmetology at the local tech college and because of her computer skills was drafted to help them with a case involving computers and identity theft. She proved to be a natural when it came to maneuvering the digital universe. Hairdressing aside, her computer skills, her willingness to plug away until she got answers, and her cheery manner had impressed Lew, who persuaded her to switch majors and study law enforcement. She was three months into an internship needed to graduate.

The only thing Lew hadn't influenced Dani to change was her hair: the girl had a head of the most explosive curls Osborne had ever seen.

"What time do we start?"

"I'd like to be at the clinic when they open at eight."

Osborne checked his watch, "We should go up. You must be exhausted."

"Maybe."

He loved that.

Chapter Seven

Osborne hurried to keep up with Lew as she headed down the hall leading to the administrative offices of the Northwoods Medical Clinic. A brass plate on the first door to the left announced it was the one she was looking for: "James McNeil, Chief Executive Officer." The door was closed.

Just as she reached for the doorknob, Lew heard a sound and paused. She turned toward Osborne, a question in her eyes. Only moments ago the receptionist at the front desk had checked with McNeil before directing them toward his office saying that the CEO was expecting them and to "go right in."

"No!" The command was sharp, the speaker was female, and the voice came from behind McNeil's closed door. Osborne wondered if there might be a misbehaving Labrador retriever in the vicinity.

"Don't tell me that, Jim," said the same voice, volume escalating. "You can't mean that. What? What? I don't believe you!"

"Whoa," said Lew under her breath. "We better wait a minute." She backed into the hall as if the emotion on the other side of the door might blow through.

If the woman sounded distraught, it was a distress tempered with belligerence. The low murmur of a male voice had followed each outcry but Osborne couldn't make out the words. Reassurance perhaps? Placating?

The woman's demanding tone sounded all too familiar to Osborne, prompting a flashback of his late wife. Mary Lee had excelled at confrontation: a stew of wounded pouts and accusing shrieks spiked with intervals of sobbing until he would feel so beaten down he would acquiesce just to shut her up.

That was why he had retired before he wanted to, why he had spent too much money on landscaping for a lake house already cosseted by elegant pines, why he had known better than to spend a dime doing something he wanted and she didn't—such as exploring the world of fly fishing—which he did not dare to do until she was gone.

The voice behind McNeil's door hurt his stomach.

The office door slammed open and a flurry of orange and black barreled toward them like a sedan with all four doors open. The woman was tall, wide shouldered, and buxom. Her dark auburn hair was tucked behind her ears, exposing a fleshy face splotched red— though it was the black V-neck top over the dizzily patterned long skirt that left the most distinct impression. Or was it the bouncing body parts exposed by the V?

"What—" Angry eyes raked Lew and Osborne up and down. "What the hell do *you* want?" As Osborne and Lew stood stunned, she whipped around and, high heels clicking a fierce staccato on the marble floor, disappeared down the hallway.

"Oh, golly, folks, sorry about that. I wasn't expecting Dr. Daniels," said the man whose tall, lean frame, emphasized by a well-fitting pinstripe business suit, now filled the doorway. He met their stare with his eyebrows lifted and head down as if ducking a flying object. "Human behavior in organizations—one of the pleasures of management."

McNeil had an open friendly face, well tanned under a youthful shock of shiny black hair slightly graying along the sideburns. And he was tall, very tall. Maybe six five, thought Osborne.

Grinning in apology as he thrust a welcoming hand toward each of them, he said, "Chief Ferris and Dr. Osborne, I'm Jim McNeil. Pleased to meet you—were you waiting long?" He gave a wan smile as if he wished he could recoup the previous few minutes and probably wondered how much they had heard.

"No, not really," said Lew.

"Well, good." McNeil did not sound convinced that his "good" was the right word. "Come in, come in. Please," he said, gesturing for each of them to take a seat in one of the chairs in front of his desk. "I want to know what I can do. Jen was one of our best and we are all of us shocked to hear this terrible news. Tell you the truth, after watching the news last night, I didn't get much sleep."

As he spoke, the color had drained from his face and he reached for a pen, which he tapped on the desk. Tapped and tapped again. A darkness hiding behind the friendly eyes told Osborne the feelings were genuine. The man was stricken: by grief or by fear.

Jim McNeil was someone Osborne knew by sight only. According to the McDonald's crowd, the relatively new CEO was in his early forties and building a good reputation among the residents of Loon Lake. The Midwest clinic was a sprawling medical center that had been completed five years earlier and was designed to replace the aging St. Mary's Hospital, whose buildings dated back to 1903. The clinic was a lifesaver for the little town of Loon Lake, as it drew patients from all across northern Wisconsin and the Upper Peninsula of Michigan, which helped to offset the slow seasons when tourism dropped.

"I appreciate your time so early this morning, Mr. McNeil," said Lew, pulling out her notepad.

"Jim," McNeil corrected her. "Dr. Osborne—have we met? Your name sounds familiar."

"I don't believe so," said Osborne, "I'm retired from a dental practice here in town."

"*That's* how I heard your name," said McNeil with a smile. "You retired too soon. When my wife and I learned we were moving up here, our dentist in Milwaukee gave you a glowing recommendation."

"Well, wasn't that nice," said Osborne, embarrassed but pleased. He did his best to avoid puffing up like a self-important ruffed grouse.

"My department is fortunate," said Lew, sounding anxious to get down to business. "Dr. Osborne is more than generous with his time. Since we have no forensic odontologist in the region even, Dr. Osborne pinch-hits as deputy coroner when I need help. The Wausau Crime Lab leans on him once in a while, too.

"Right now, with yesterday's tragedy on top of this being the height of the tourist season and all the problems that brings—I've deputized Dr. Osborne to assist with the investigation." She gave a slight smile and said, "Loon Lake is a small town and I am chronically short-staffed."

"I kno-o-w the feeling," said McNeil. Another ingratiating grin.

He's a charmer, thought Osborne. Good people person. Glancing around the room, Osborne noted McNeil had a pronounced masculine taste—or the clinic's decorator did: the walls hung with framed prints of ducks flying, deer in snowdrifts, and an etching of a black bear. Along the east side of the room, a wall of windows looked out over the grounds of the clinic and the rear parking lot used by employees.

"I must tell you I still cannot get over the fact that Jen has been . . ." said McNeil, his voice trailing off before he said, "do you have any idea—"

"Not yet," said Lew, stepping on his words. "That's why we're here. I'm hoping someone she worked with may know something that could help us. How familiar were *you* with Jennifer if I might ask?"

"Well, I certainly knew her," said McNeil. "She ran our graphics department—did a swell job with brochures, newsletters, special publications. She was an artist. In fact, we were just at a marketing conference in Madison and the collateral materials she designed for our clinic were every bit as good as what the big boys have. Jennifer was a real pro."

"What about her personality? Did she get along with people?" asked Lew.

"That I can't answer. We had a supervisory relationship and you know how that goes—people are always on their best behavior with the boss."

The smile this time seemed a little tight to Osborne. He made an "x" on his notepad and wrote the word "smile" with a question mark alongside.

"I've made up a list of people with whom we would like to talk this morning if possible," said Lew, handing over a sheet of paper. "Jennifer's mother, Bonnie, made these suggestions."

McNeil studied the handwritten list of names.

"I would add a few," he said. "Jen was good at connecting with all the department chairs and their staff. I suggest you check with several people whom I know have worked with her recently. Let me give this some thought then I'll have my secretary call you if that's okay? She can reach you faster than I can. Too many meetings."

"I would appreciate that," said Lew. "The first person I would like to question is Kerry Schultz, one of your nurses."

"Of course," said McNeil. "I see you have her on your list. But Dr. Daniels?" he asked. "Jen had minimal interaction with Cynthia Daniels—that I'm aware of."

"Oh, you know," said Lew, waving one hand airily, "that's a name her mom mentioned. Just touching base with everyone. You never know, you know."

"I doubt Dr. Daniels has time unless you insist. She's a surgeon in our trauma center. One of our emergency medicine specialists. That's one hardworking specialty—often on call, they work nights. As far as the rest of these, if you'll hold on, I'll have my secretary arrange a conference room for you and get folks organized so you can see everyone today if possible."

"Thank you, Mr. McNeil," said Lew, rising from her chair.

"Jim," said McNeil, pumping her hand with enthusiasm and handing her a business card. "Call me, Jim, please, Chief Ferris. And do not hesitate to touch base if you have more questions—easiest to reach me after hours."

Lew glanced down at the card he handed her. "Is this your home phone number?" She sounded surprised. "Your wife isn't Leigh Richards by any chance?"

"Yes. Why?"

"I thought your phone number looked familiar. She has called nine-one-one twice in the last few weeks to report a prowler on your property. I've had my officers assigned to drive past your home during their night patrols but they haven't reported seeing anyone. Have you had any more disturbances?"

Inflating his cheeks with a deep exhale, McNeil said, "I'll check that out with Leigh. Again. She insists someone is coming on our property but I haven't seen anyone. Believe me, you would hear from me, too, if I did. Of course, each time this has happened, I have been away on a business trip so it's possible. . . ."

He hesitated then said, "My wife is a lovely, wonderful woman but she gets lonely and, frankly, hears bumps in the night. Know what I mean? I will remind her that your police officers are keeping an eye out for us. That is sure to relieve her worries."

He walked them toward his office door. "My secretary, Amy, is right around the corner, Chief Ferris. If you will stop by her desk, she'll set things up for you and Dr. Osborne. Again, please call me if you have any more questions, need anything—if there is any way myself or the clinic can help, I want to be sure we do so."

"Nice man," said Lew as they walked toward the secretary's office.

"Worried man," said Osborne. "Very . . . worried . . . man."

"Really?" Lew turned puzzled eyes on him. "That's why I like having you along, Doc. You hear things I don't."

Chapter Eight

"Oh, yes, Jen and I've been buds since she started working here," said Kerry Schultz in answer to a question from Lew. Her voice grew hoarse as she tried to speak saying, "We . . . um . . . we worked out at the Y together three times a week."

She wiped at a tear and tried to smile. "We joked that neither one of us could do the elliptical if we were alone—we needed gossip to take our minds off the damn thing." She hesitated, "Jen was in much better shape than me. You know, Jen . . . oh . . ."

It was a losing battle. Tears filled her eyes and she reached for a Kleenex from a box on her desk in the cubicle provided for the head of the surgical nursing team. Lew and Osborne sat quietly as she tried to compose herself.

Kerry was petite, small-boned, and, if you believed the crisp, green scrubs she was wearing, which did not compliment her waistline—plump around the edges. Her cap of wispy yolk-yellow hair gleamed in the sunlight streaming through the clinic windows. When she lifted her face from the Kleenex, almond-shaped hazel eyes set off an expanse of lightly-tanned skin scattered with freckles and devoid of makeup.

It was a face that reminded Osborne of a field of prairie grasses: wide open, dappled, and refreshingly plain. A face that encouraged him to trust what she might say.

"Was she dating anyone?" asked Lew.

"Umm . . . not really," said Kerry. Her eyes darted off for a second as if she was rethinking that answer. "No, no, she wasn't . . . dating . . . any one."

Lew waited for a long moment, then said, "Is there anything you would add to that?"

Kerry shook her head as she blinked hard to hold back tears. She blew her nose. The cubicle was quiet.

"I see," said Lew, "actually, I'm surprised. I'm under the impression Jen was quite an attractive young woman—"

"So am I," said Kerry with an apologetic little grin. "And I'm not dating anyone either. Hard to meet guys in Loon Lake—even Rhinelander is barren territory. Half the time you grew up with them and know they're total razzbonyas or they're new in town and already attached." She sniffed.

None of this was news to Osborne—he'd heard plenty on the subject of men and dating from Erin and Mallory.

"Well, in that case," said Lew, "what can you tell us about Jennifer's outside interests? Away from the clinic and besides working out at the Y? Other people she did things with? Other close friends?"

"I think I was her best friend," said Kerry. "We'd go to movies together. Kayak on the weekends if the weather was nice, maybe go for a swim at my folks' place. That was pretty much it. Oh, well, we did drive down to Wausau for shopping a couple times, and on the Fourth of July we hosted a pontoon party together."

Kerry managed a smile. "That got kind of wild. The party, I mean. Not our fault—one of the guys at the party had too much to drink, went overboard, and passed out. I did CPR, but we had to call nine-one-one—just to be sure he was okay. I'm sure the EMTs thought we were all plowed but I wasn't. Jen wasn't either. Still, the story got around town. . . ." She glanced at Lew, "I imagine you heard the worst?"

"That one escaped me," said Lew with an easy grin. "The Fourth is one of our busiest holidays of the year. More serious shenanigans to worry about than over-served partygoers. Back to Jennifer—you're saying there were no men in her life?"

"I didn't say *that*," said Kerry. "Jen went out with a bunch of different guys when she first moved here. 'Inappropriate boy friends' is what she got a kick out of calling them. Once she got to know them, she didn't like their lifestyle—too much drinking, smoking."

"'Jack pine savages?'" asked Osborne in a humorous tone.

"Not *that* bad," said Kerry with a wince. "It's just . . . she was easily disappointed."

"High standards?" said Lew.

"That's a good way to put it. Jen was ambitious. She wanted a guy who was going somewhere. I suppose I can be crass and say she wanted someone who would make money."

"Like a doctor?"

"Yes," said Kerry, "like a doctor. But good luck with that—the ones on staff here are either married or . . . not very attractive. Sorry if I sound mean."

"You sound like a couple of discerning young women to me," said Lew. She turned to Osborne, "Doc—your turn."

"When *was* the last time she dated anyone?" asked Osborne.

"You think it was a man who did this?" asked Kerry.

"We don't know yet," said Lew, "but in my experience attacks of this nature tend to be crimes of passion. Your friend died of a single deep stab wound. Possibly premeditated. And I say that because it appears the killer was skilled at wielding a knife."

Worry flashed across Kerry's face. "What—" asked Lew.

"Nothing," said Kerry. "Maybe I'm forgetting something, but I am sure it's been a year or more since she dated anyone, and even though she dumped the guy, I don't remember her saying that he bothered her afterward."

"And who was that?"

"Bart Martin."

"He just got married, right?"

"Yeah, I can't imagine he would . . . Actually, he's my cousin, and I can't see him doing that to Jen. I just can't."

Lew looked down at her list of questions before saying, "So as far as you know, Jen wasn't active in any groups like a pool league or a volleyball team. Did she golf? Play bunco? What about knitting or quilting?"

"Jen was more of a loner than a lot of the gals here."

"Did she like to fish?" asked Osborne even as he knew it was a ridiculous question.

"No-o-o, but I'll tell you what she *did* do a lot in her spare time: watercolors. She was working on watercolors of dragonflies that she was planning to sell at the art fair in Eagle River during Cranberry Fest." Kerry nodded as if she had found the right answer: "Yep, Jen spent a lot of time painting."

Kerry's pager buzzed suddenly. She checked the message. "Looks like I'm being called into our weekly meeting with the emergency room staff. Afraid I better scoot."

"One last question," said Lew. "Did Jen work well with people here at the clinic?"

"I would say so," said Kerry, her eyes thoughtful. "Everyone I know liked her. She was very easy to work with—she ran the graphics department and always said her job was to make us all look good."

"What about Cynthia Daniels?" asked Lew.

"Oh, her," Kerry waved a dismissive hand. "No one likes her. She's a pain in the butt. I doubt she would say anything good about Jen—or me for that matter. Not sure what her problem is but . . . Why do you ask about Dr. Daniels?"

"Can you give us an example of what you mean when you say Dr. Daniels has nothing good to say about you or Jen?" asked Osborne.

He had learned in his own practice that dental assistants, dental hygienists, even receptionists, often had the most accurate read on the professionals—and the patients—with whom they worked.

Kerry tipped her head sideways and chewed the inside of her right cheek before saying, "This is between us, right?"

"Unless it has a direct bearing on who may have murdered Jennifer Williams," said Lew.

"It doesn't. When Dr. Cynthia Daniels makes a mistake—no matter how big or small—she finds someone else to blame. She's a slacker, too. Makes like she works her tail off in the ER all the time but she doesn't. To put it bluntly: the woman's sloppy. And she's a bitch."

Kerry grinned, "Aren't you glad you asked? Now—why she developed such a dislike for Jen, I don't know. Their paths rarely crossed except," she paused and the flash of worry crossed her face once more, "except when entering and leaving the clinic." Kerry's pager buzzed again and she stood up. "Will you be talking to Dr. Daniels?"

"She told Mr. McNeil's secretary she doesn't have time today," said Lew.

"Really?" Kerry looked surprised. "Well, chances are she'll be in this meeting I'm going to. Why don't you come along and pull her out of the meeting? It's nothing critical—just our weekly update on schedules—she misses it half the time anyway. Tell her I said I'll take notes for her."

A devilish smile crinkled Kerry's eyes. "Just 'cause you're a doctor doesn't mean you're a nice person, you know. Ask *her* why she didn't like Jen. I'm interested in what she says."

Cynthia Daniels was seated on the far side of the room that they entered. She sat with her legs crossed and the long skirt hiked up to expose long, tanned legs. Engrossed in the pages of a magazine in her lap, she didn't notice Lew and Osborne enter the room and stand against the back wall.

Other staff members filed in and were taking their seats on folding chairs when Lew raised her voice to call across the room, "Dr. Daniels? Dr. Osborne and I would like to speak with you, please."

"Sorry," said the woman, recrossing her legs. "Afraid I'm busy all today. Right now I'm needed in this meeting. Tomorrow maybe. You can check with my secretary. Brenda. Down the hall that way." Cynthia flipped a hand toward the door.

"That's okay, Dr. Daniels, I'll take notes for you," said Kerry, seated in a chair on the other side of the room. She gave Cynthia a cheery smile.

The tall, middle-aged man at the front of the room who appeared to be the person running the meeting said, "Go ahead, Dr. Daniels. This will be short today anyway." He glanced at his watch. "You aren't scheduled in ER until four this afternoon so take your time."

Cynthia glowered.

Chapter Nine

Shoulders set like a tight end for the Green Bay Packers and elbows pumping, Cynthia Daniels stormed past the cramped cubby that fronted her office door. Barreling through the doorway, she disappeared. Osborne waited, expecting the door to be slammed behind her. He was disappointed.

Crouched in a corner of the cubby and ignored by Cynthia as she flew by, was a plain-faced young woman with lank brown hair crammed into a clip stuck high on the back of her head. She flinched as Cynthia swung past, and Osborne sensed that the physician's unexpected return had just ruined the girl's morning.

"Brenda—" Cynthia's voice from behind the wall was muffled but imperious. "Get me a coffee. Black." The young woman jumped to her feet. She threw a questioning glance toward Lew and Osborne who had followed Cynthia down the hall only to come to a skidding halt beside the cubby.

"Nothing for us, thank you," said Lew, her words as kind as Cynthia's had been rude. The girl scurried off, shoulders hunched, leaving Osborne and Lew to stand outside Cynthia's office.

"Hello?" asked Lew after a long moment. She made sure her voice was loud enough to carry into the next room.

Not a word in response. No welcome, not even a grudging acknowledgment of their presence. Lew cut her eyes sideways, signaling "watch out for flying objects" before walking through the open doorway. Osborne followed.

The office was modest in its dimensions but felt spacious thanks to a wall of windows facing south toward the mid-morning sun. The windows had been cracked open a few inches to let a warm morning breeze flow in.

As if to save space, the office was designed with a desktop running along the east wall and cabinets cantilevered overhead. Two upholstered armchairs were set under the windows with a small table between them. A low bookcase lined the wall just inside the door. The top of the bookcase held a small red fox caught mid-run. Osborne recognized the animal as the handiwork of a taxidermist he had known well: Cynthia's late father.

"So this is your office?" asked Lew in an effort to make conversation as they entered.

"Not an examining room," was the curt response from the woman seated in a large swivel armchair, which was turned away from them toward the desk. The desk was heaped with files, loose papers, empty Styrofoam cups, and a laptop computer with a smudged screen. A mess of a workplace, thought Osborne, wondering how often Cynthia lost or mislaid patient records.

Then he reminded himself: everything is electronic these days. Cynthia Daniels could make as big a mess as she wanted to and not kill anyone. At least he hoped that was how the clinic worked.

Not until after Lew and Osborne had entered the room and stood waiting did Cynthia spin around to face them. She crossed her legs and yanked on her skirt until it fell below her knee—though not far enough to interfere with the impatient pumping of her left foot. Her gesture toward two empty chairs was more a surrender than a welcome.

Averting his eyes from the nervous foot—and the twin globes showcased in the black V-neck top—Osborne focused on the skirt, which was patterned with fat orange birds adorned with bright green butterfly wings outlined in black. He wasn't sure what made him queasier: the ugly skirt or the pumping foot. A *large* pumping foot wearing a black stiletto heel that must come in men's sizes. Nothing about Cynthia was modest—in size or effect.

The woman in the swivel chair stared at Lew and Osborne, then raised her chin and bared her teeth in what was intended to pass as a smile. Osborne didn't read it that way. She reminded him of chimpanzees he had studied back in his dental school psych class: the ones determined to exhibit dominance over the group.

She needn't have gone to the effort. When Osborne sat down in one of the chairs in front of the windows, he discovered the chair sat so low, he had to look up, way up, if he wanted to make eye contact with Cynthia. Ah, intimidation by chair. He caught Lew's eye. She grinned.

"All right, you have my undivided attention—so . . . *what.*"

It was less a question than a demand as she crossed her arms. "What do you need to know that everyone else here can't tell you a hell of a lot better than I can because I didn't even *know* Jennifer Williams? Such a waste of my time." The hostility in the woman's voice chilled the room in spite of the morning breezes.

"You," she said to Osborne in a dismissive tone. "You look familiar. You the chief of police? I feel like we've met. Treated you in ER, maybe?"

Osborne took pleasure (unfair, he knew, but he couldn't resist) in extending his hand and maintaining a gracious tone as he said, "No, Cynthia, I was your father's dentist—before he passed away. Years ago when you were just a little tyke, your folks lived in our neighborhood.

"In fact, I was admiring your wonderful fox there. I'd left one with your dad hoping to get a nice mount just like it but he never got round to it before he passed away. Your dad did fine taxidermy."

"So you knew Marv and Gladys," said Cynthia, giving his hand a limp shake.

Marv and Gladys, thought Osborne, *right.* Years ago it had irritated him that she called her parents (and her parents' adult friends such as himself and Mary Lee) by their first names. Still did.

Sitting back in the low chair, Osborne said, "These days I am retired from my practice but I assist Chief Lewellyn Ferris here," he gestured toward Lew, "whenever an odontologist is needed for work with dental records—or as a deputy coroner. I'm sure you're familiar with the advantages of forensic dentistry. Right now, with all the summer tourism, the department is short-handed so I'm helping with the investigation."

"*You're* the chief of police?" Cynthia turned her chair toward Lew. She made no effort to hide a supercilious tone. "I didn't know women were—"

"Just like medicine," said Lew before she could finish, "we've invaded the male domain." And she smiled a smile Osborne recognized as dangerous.

"A few questions about your colleague who was murdered late yesterday afternoon," said Lew, intent on moving the conversation along and opening the long, narrow notebook resting on her knee.

"Barely knew her. I mean, I certainly knew who she *was* but that's it."

The young woman named Brenda appeared in the doorway with a cafeteria tray on which rested a mug with Cynthia's coffee and two glasses of ice water.

"Why, thank you, Brenda," said Lew as she reached for one of the glasses.

"Yes, thank you," said Osborne, taking the remaining glass. With a sigh of impatience, Cynthia reached for her coffee. As Brenda backed away through the doorway, Osborne spotted Kerry standing beside Brenda's cubby. She waved and winked.

"Brenda, close the door," said Cynthia. "Hold my calls."

"I understand you and Jennifer Williams had some difficulties working together," said Lew after the door clicked closed.

"What do you mean by that? Told you I barely knew the woman. She had no medical credentials and a bad habit of getting in the way. I had to tell her to back off more than a few times. Trauma medicine is demanding. Very demanding—and you don't need some fool poking around with a camera."

"Was she *assigned* to photograph the emergency room?" asked Lew. "Or was she interfering for no good reason?"

Cynthia shrugged. "Who knows? I'm sure it was her job, but she didn't have to get in my face."

"You're an attractive woman," said Osborne, "maybe she was told to be sure to include you in clinic advertising—like brochures and billboards. Wouldn't that make for positive advertising?"

As he spoke, he made a mental note to check with his oldest daughter, Mallory. He was pretty sure she was the same age as Cynthia, though Cynthia's parents had sent her to boarding school while Mallory attended the local high school. Be interesting to hear what Mallory might have to say.

Cynthia heaved a sigh. "I'm sure that was the case but she was a pest."

"Thank you for your time," said Lew, getting to her feet. "Since you say you didn't know her well, that about covers it."

Osborne saw a crafty look spread across Cynthia's face as she rocked back in her chair. "They told you how she was around the docs, right?" she asked Lew.

"No, I don't believe anyone has—is there something we should know?" Lew paused before reaching the doorway.

"She was, well, I'd call it promiscuous. Blatantly promiscuous," said Cynthia. "Frankly, I have no doubt her entire reason for taking the job at this clinic was to marry a doctor—or an administrator. I mean—the way she hung on Jim McNeil, for example, was . . . sinful. Even his wife got upset. Though," Cynthia rolled her eyes, "*there's* a nut case."

"Mr. McNeil?" asked Osborne.

"His wife. You heard about her, right? She's convinced people are breaking into her house. You should talk to her—ask *her* about Jennifer Williams. Poor soul is paranoid. A lit-tle over the top, too, if you ask me. I've encouraged Jim to get her some counseling."

Lew sat back down on the chair. "How do you know all this? About Mrs. McNeil being worried about intruders? Is that common knowledge here at the clinic?"

"Well . . ." Cynthia hedged with a coy look, "I certainly heard about it from Jim."

"He confides in you?" Lew's tone was noncommittal.

"We're good friends." The hostility had evaporated. Cynthia appeared pleased with herself.

"You didn't sound very friendly during your encounter this morning," said Lew. "Dr. Osborne and I were standing outside his office while you were shouting."

"Oh, that!" Cynthia waved a hand. "That was all about my schedule. We go through that every month."

"I see. One last question," said Lew. "Where were you late yesterday afternoon between five o'clock and six thirty?"

"Here. At the clinic. In the emergency room."

"And you have witnesses to corroborate that?"

Cynthia's voice tightened. "Aren't you overstepping, Mrs. Ferris? Of course, I have witnesses. Probably half the ER staff. For heaven's sakes, why?"

"It's a question we're asking everyone," said Osborne before Lew could answer. He summoned the tone he'd perfected over the years to assure dental patients that "you'll feel a pinch and that's all" as he administered a shot of Novocain.

But Cynthia's eyes had widened.

A sudden knock on the door as Brenda cracked it open, saying, "Dr. Daniels, your mother is on the phone. I told her you were meeting with the police but she insists—"

"Please, take your call," said Lew, getting to her feet for the second time. "You've answered my questions. If I have more later, Dr. Osborne or myself will be in touch."

"Gladys—what's the problem?" asked Cynthia, her voice loud and unhappy. She listened for ten seconds then waved for Lew and Osborne to wait, then listened again. "Are you serious? Okay, I'll tell them. You're home now? Yes. I will." She put the phone down and stood up.

"Well—that's a surprise," said Cynthia. "My mother lives about a half mile from those condos where Jennifer Williams was killed. She always walks the dog down that road and thinks she may have seen something yesterday. She isn't sure it's important but she wants you to call her. Said she'll be home all afternoon."

Cynthia reached for a small notepad and a pen on her desk. She scribbled something quickly and handed the note to Lew. "Here's her cell phone number—she doesn't answer the house phone."

Lew glanced down at the number and said, "Your mother doesn't wear a purple coat by any chance?"

"Yes, she does. Why?"

"We're trying to reach all the residents in the area and we were told there was an elderly woman in a purple coat walking a small dog right around the time that Jennifer may have been attacked."

"That would be Gladys," said Cynthia. "She has a Yorkie."

"This has been very helpful, thank you for your time," said Lew, reaching to shake Cynthia's hand.

"Sure," said Cynthia, more agreeable than she had been all morning. Osborne noticed the hand she extended to Lew was shaking.

Chapter Ten

As they left Cynthia's office, Brenda jumped to her feet, motioning for them to follow her down the hall. After leading the way through double doors requiring a passkey and down another long hallway, she beckoned them into a small waiting area.

"Chief Ferris," said Brenda, sounding more confident than she had all morning, "I heard you ask Dr. Daniels where she was yesterday afternoon. I thought you should know she was *not* in the emergency room. She wasn't in the doctors' lounge either. I know because she had an emergency call from the clinic in Minocqua and I could not find her. I even had her paged and she didn't answer."

"Why would she say she was here if she wasn't?" asked Lew.

"I have no idea," said Brenda. "She only works thirty-six hours a week and she wasn't on call yesterday either. And she lies a lot."

"She *lies*?" asked Lew. "Dr. Daniels *lies*? What kind of lies? Can you give us an example?"

Brenda shrugged, her face impassive. "She'll make a mistake. Maybe something dangerous for the patient and blame someone else even though she did it. A good friend of mine who's a nurse in the ER has seen her do it. Oh, and sometimes she fakes that she's sick when she isn't. I know she isn't 'cause I'll see her fixing her makeup to go meet someone."

"You don't care much for her, do you?" asked Lew.

Brenda gave a tight little smile of satisfaction as she said, "Today is my last day working here. I put in for a transfer a couple months ago—so I start at the clinic in Rhinelander next week. Just so you know, I'm not the first to ask for a transfer away from her. Dr. Daniels is not a nice person.

"But men like her," she said, raising her eyebrows in wonderment. "The men here *adore* her."

Lew caught her eye and nodded, "And we know why, don't we." Brenda chuckled, then checked her watch.

"Do you need to get back?" asked Osborne.

"Umm, not really. I'm on break. It's okay."

"Brenda, did *you* know Jennifer Williams?" asked Lew.

"Oh sure. I really like Jen. She's pretty cool. She always wears . . . Oops, sorry, I mean *wore* the coolest jeans and carried these really funky purses." She paused, her eyes glistening, "I—we—all of us here . . ." She took a deep breath, "We can't believe what happened." A long pause, then Brenda whispered, "But, umm, Dr. Daniels just hated her. I shouldn't say this but I'll bet she's glad Jen's . . . gone."

"Any good reason why?" asked Lew. "That you could see?"

"Um . . . no," said Brenda, shaking her head. The "no" was so hesitant Lew and Osborne exchanged glances.

"It's okay, Brenda," said Osborne, doing his best to sound fatherly. "Chief Ferris and I have heard other people mention that Dr. Daniels didn't care for Jen. We're just exploring all the reasons why that might be. No one is accusing anyone."

"They'll deny it, I'm sure, but Mr. McNeil and Dr. Daniels have been having an affair. I'm not sure, but I think he's been trying to weasel out of it." Brenda gave a harsh laugh and said, "Dr. Daniels doesn't know this but she's not the only one he's fooled around with. He's the type—know what I mean? I feel sorry for his wife."

"Was he involved with Jennifer? Is *that* what you mean?" asked Lew.

"Oh no, I don't think so. I mean someone else." Brenda leaned forward to whisper, "Corrine Jensen. But that was last summer."

"Is the relationship between Mr. McNeil and Dr. Daniels common knowledge?" asked Lew.

Brenda nodded. "I'm not sure. I've known—and Kerry Schultz and some of the other nurses. But if you need proof, I've been her assistant for the last year and I've had access to her e-mails. All the ones she sent Mr. McNeil—I've saved. And some he sent her." Brenda smirked.

"Was this in case she tried to have you fired?" asked Lew.

"Yeah. My dad told me to. He's a retired cop—from Chicago."

"But Brenda," said Osborne, "let's back up for a moment. Why Cynthia Daniels's intense dislike of Jennifer? Does it make sense to you?"

"She was jealous," said Brenda. "For one thing, everyone liked Jen. Especially Mr. McNeil. He would go out of his way to say nice things about her work in his Monday morning clinic newsletter. Just last week he went on and on about how our clinic's brochures and posters all won awards at some big conference. Dr. Daniels did not like *that*. Not one bit."

Back at the cruiser, Lew slid onto the driver's seat, cell phone in hand, and punched in the number that Cynthia had given her. After reaching the elderly woman who answered and arranging with Gladys to meet at her home later that afternoon, she clicked off.

"Doc, I'd say Cynthia Daniels just may learn a hard lesson."

"And what is that?" asked Osborne, looking forward to the answer.

"Don't kick the little guy."

As she turned the key in the ignition, Lew's police radio gave an alert.

"Marlaine?" she said to the switchboard operator who was on the line, "can this wait? Doc and I are on our way to the station right now—oh, all right, go ahead." Lew tipped her head, listening. Marlaine being a large woman with a voice that boomed made it easy for Osborne to hear her every word even as he sat over in the passenger seat.

"First, Chief Ferris, I thought you would like to know that Bruce Peters got here an hour ago and is working the crime scene. . . ."

"Good. But is that why you called?" asked Lew. She glanced at Osborne—that was one piece of information that could have waited five minutes.

"No. Chief, I've got a very upset individual here at the station insisting we put out an APB for his truck that he says was stolen by a friend of his."

Lew rolled her eyes. "Well, did you tell him we don't do APB's on stolen vehicles?"

"I tried. He says he'll lose his job if we can't find it for him. Said he loaned it to Alvin Marski yesterday who promised to return it last night. Chief, he's *very* upset."

"Okay," said Lew with a sigh, "tell him I'll be there shortly and we'll discuss it then. Is that it?"

"Yes, it's just the guy is losing it and I wanted you to be prepared."

"Thanks, Marlaine. See you in a minute."

Clicking off the phone, Lew said, "Alvin Marski. Great. There's a guy with a rap sheet of misdemeanors way longer than our pal Ray Pradt. Specializes in petty theft—gas cans out of boats, little kids' Halloween candy. Stealing a vehicle doesn't sound like Alvin, although last fall I nailed him for growing weed in his mother's backyard. She insisted it was hers—if you can believe it. Poor woman. I'm sure that jabone's half way to Detroit by now."

"Is that Rhonda Marski's son?" asked Osborne, remembering the exhausted but sweet woman, a widow who cleaned houses and spent money she couldn't afford when her teenaged son had to have his front teeth replaced after losing them in a fight. Osborne charged her all of twenty-five dollars for the work. He couldn't bear sending the poor soul a bill for close to a thousand.

Alvin, good-looking kid born under the sign of bad behavior.

"We got a call from the Loon Lake Pharmacy where he's been buying too much Sudafed recently," said Lew. "I don't think he's *cooking* meth but he's got friends with bad ideas."

Preoccupied as he pulled past the screen of pine trees fronting his driveway, Osborne was startled to see two mountain bikes parked in front of the garage door. He hit the brakes just in time.

Beth must have ridden home for lunch. With a friend. Either that or the kid was capable of riding two bikes at once. Sure enough, as Mike charged toward him across the yard, he heard a girlish voice call up from down near the dock.

"Grandpa . . . Harry and I are down here. Okay?"

"Sure," said Osborne, heading down the rock staircase toward the water.

Recalling Lew's caution that Beth's constant text messaging was likely to involve a boy, he steeled himself to perform as a good grandfather should. Given he had raised two daughters now functioning as capable adults, he must know *something* about how to handle young people. At least he hoped.

"My friend Harry borrowed one of your spinning rods, okay, Gramps? Not a good one—the one you let Cody use," she said, speaking fast and referring to her kid brother.

"That's fine. How long have you been here? Nice to meet you, Harry," he said, walking onto the dock to join the two teenagers.

Beth was tall and willowy with the same flaxen hair as her mother. Harry was nearly six feet and quite skinny with a shock of straight light brown hair that did a good job of hiding his eyes. *Kid needs a haircut* was Osborne's first thought.

"Harry, how did you manage to make the girls' basketball team?" said Osborne, walking up to the boy, extending a hand, and smiling at his own joke. "What's your last name, son?"

"The boys' clinic is over in the junior high gym," said Beth, jumping in a little too fast.

"Harry Gardner. We . . . um . . . Beth and I have to get back for afternoon practice but we thought maybe it was all right to have our sandwiches out here?" His voice rose, leaving his question hanging in the air.

"Sure," said Osborne. "I don't mind but will you kids let the dog into the house before you leave? I'm going to make myself a quick bite to eat and skedaddle. Beth, did your mother bring your things by?" Osborne wondered why *he* felt awkward.

"Yes. She left a note for you on the kitchen table."

"And when do you get out of practice this afternoon?"

"Um . . . four o'clock?" This time it was Beth's voice ending on a high note. "But Harry and I—we—we're going to bike the Bearskin for an hour. . . ."

"Really? Aren't you going to be exhausted after basketball practice?" asked Osborne. "I don't mind if you go for a bike ride, but don't overdo it in this heat, young lady."

"I won't, Grandpa. The coaches want us to either run or bike an hour a day before or after practice."

"Your mother didn't mention that."

The two kids stared at him. Osborne backed off. "Okay, that's fine. Just so you're back here by five-thirty. Maybe you and I will go out in the boat? Lew might join us. Harry, you look like a fisherman—want to come along?"

"You bet I would," said the boy. "I know this lake—my dad fishes it with a buddy of his. You got trophy muskies in here, Dr. Osborne."

"You're right, we do," said Doc. "See you two later, then."

Walking back up to the house, he wondered if Beth appreciated the fact his trophy muskie lake might lure a boy or two. His granddaughter was an attractive girl, but let's be real: big fish count too, doncha know.

The thought made him happy in spite of the dread he had felt ever since Lew asked him to join her in questioning Gladys Daniels.

Gladys Daniels: one of the few people in Loon Lake who frightened him.

Chapter Eleven

A lush lawn, mowed with precision, swept along Bobcat Lane, all the way from where it turned off the county road to where it ended in a circle drive fronting the brick and stone mansion owned by the Daniels family. Buttery daylilies in full bloom filled the center of the circular drive, the blooms bouncing off one another in the summer breezes.

A pitched roof of dark gray shake shingles guarded the front entry, and a granite chimney anchored the far end of the house. Along the right side of the lane a wall of stately pines fended off inquisitive neighbors.

Built in the early 1900s as a summer home for a dairy magnate from Chicago, the house was a landmark coveted by the wives of Loon Lake's professional men—including Osborne's late wife. Gladys Daniels had scored quite a coup when she and her husband bought the property from the widow of the retired boat manufacturer who had owned the home.

According to Mary Lee and her bridge group, Gladys had cheated her way into ownership by convincing the soon-to-be bereaved widow that she would be short of money unless she sold the home to Gladys and Marvin *before* her husband's death—a transaction that Gladys swore would allow the family to avoid tens of thousands of dollars in real estate taxes.

She had exaggerated the tax issue—or as Mary Lee put it: "She *lied*!" But that didn't surface until months after the purchase had gone through. Everyone knew it was Gladys, not Marvin, behind the scheme. The ladies took their revenge: she was banned from the bridge table, and it was a decade before she was allowed back into the Loon Lake Garden Club.

Gladys could not have cared less. Shoulders back and smile fixed, she was mistress of one of the most elegant homes in the Northwoods. That was all that mattered.

Before Osborne could raise his right hand to knock, the front door swung open. Though he had seldom run into the woman in the years since her husband's death, he could see at a glance that Gladys Daniels was proof some things never change.

She had to be well into her seventies but the helmet of curls salon-pressed to her head remained ink black. Her face was still an unnatural white under a mask of foundation, the makeup flaking along the lines of her jowls. Her eyes, rimmed with mascara, were dark and hard as ever ("pinpoints of evil" according to his daughter Mallory, who had been at the butt end of Gladys's gossip the summer after her junior year of high school), and the usual scarlet slash marked her lips.

A buxom woman with spindly legs, today Gladys was wearing a dark purple blouse that reached to her mid-section where it hung over slacks of the same shade. Pale arms protruding from elbow-length sleeves held a small, yapping dog with long hair whose beady eyes, not unlike those of his mistress, peered out from below a topknot tied with a purple ribbon that matched its owner's blouse.

"Hello, Paul," said Gladys without breaking a smile. She had a reedy, nasal voice pitched high—an echo of Cynthia's shrill ultimatums Osborne had overheard while standing outside Jim McNeil's office that morning.

"Come in, you two." It was less a welcome than a demand. The heavy wooden door swung wide.

Gladys stepped back into a dark foyer while Osborne waited for Lew to enter ahead of him. "I imagine *you're* the chief of police my daughter told me about?" Eyebrows arched, Gladys made it obvious both she and Cynthia had a hard time believing *that* to be a fact.

"Yes," said Lew, ignoring the put-down. "I'm Chief Lewellyn Ferris with the Loon Lake Police, and I understand you already know Dr. Osborne," Lew gestured toward Osborne as she spoke, then said, "and we appreciate you're taking the time to meet with us, Mrs. Daniels.

"When we spoke with Dr. Daniels earlier, she indicated you were out walking yesterday and may have seen someone in the vicinity of the crime?"

"About that in a minute," said Gladys. "Of course I know *Paul*." She managed to make his name sound as if it tasted bad. "Cynthia tried explaining why on earth he has to be here. I don't understand what some . . . *dentist* has to do with this? And *Paul* of all people?" In spite of her ill humor, she pointed the way down a short, dark hallway.

"Well, Gladys, Chief Ferris has deputized me because—"

Before Osborne could utter another word, she interrupted saying, "Paul, I haven't seen you since Marvin passed. Why is that?" She paused and turned to glare at him.

"Well, I—"

"Never mind." Again a dismissive wave as she turned away. "Mary Lee was the only one in your family who knew the proper way to do things." Resisting the urge to defend his daughters, Osborne said nothing—preferring to note that as she spoke, Gladys appeared to be squeezing the life out of the dog squirming in the crook of her left arm.

They entered a cavernous, formal living room where the French windows along one wall were hung with drapes so heavy they allowed only a hint of afternoon sun. Walking behind the two women, it struck Osborne that while they might be the same height, that was where similarities ended.

One was sturdy and muscular in her summer uniform of crisp khaki, the fabric of her shirt and pants defining the breasts and hips that he had come to know so well. Her skin was tanned and glowing beneath an untamed cluster of nut-brown curls. In the dim light of the stuffy room, Lewellyn Ferris was a breath of fresh air.

Gladys, scuttling along in the shiny purple shirt, one skinny arm waving, brought to mind an insect: an iridescent beetle with spidery limbs. Unkind to think that, he knew, but Osborne couldn't help it.

"Sit down over there, you two."

Following orders, Osborne and Lew sat down, side by side, on a beige brocade love seat with curved wooden legs. Osborne let himself down onto the small sofa with care, not sure it was sturdy enough to hold them both . . . but it seemed stable.

Gladys settled herself and the dog into a large wingchair across from them. To her right was an ornate mahogany library table holding a porcelain table lamp made from a Chinese vase and crowned with a cream-colored fringed shade. The dog gave a yap of protest as Gladys pressed it onto her lap.

Her blunt, officious manner prompted Osborne to wonder (not for the first time) how such a mean-spirited woman had managed to attract good-natured Marvin, a man with whom Osborne had spent many pleasant hours in the fishing boat back when they were neighbors and shortly after Cynthia had been born.

Marvin Daniels was the kind of man who would go out of his way to shovel the porch and sidewalk for the elderly couple living next door to them, and would not hesitate to stop by with jumper cables whenever a neighbor's car battery died in the depths of winter. And it was Marvin who always made sure to buy Girl Scout cookies from the neighbor children—no matter how many knocked on their door.

The two men had met when Osborne and Mary Lee bought their first home on a side street in Loon Lake. The Daniels family lived on the same block. At the time, it was a neighborhood ritual for the husbands to gather one Thursday evening a month for an evening of beer and poker. Marvin, a manager at the paper mill, was a regular.

Or he was until the night Gladys barged in, grabbed him by the ear (literally), and hauled him out. Osborne and the other husbands had watched in stunned silence. No excuse was ever given as to what Marvin may have done to precipitate his wife's anger, but he never showed up for Thursday night poker again.

That was just the beginning. Next Gladys forced him to resign from the Lions Club; then she put the kibosh on his spending all night at the Flowage followed by pancakes with the guys at Pete's Place—the annual celebration of opening fishing season. Over the coming years, Marvin did manage to eke out a few days of walleye fishing, but only when Gladys and Cynthia were off shopping in Green Bay.

In fairness to Gladys, Mary Lee had pointed out that she did approve of golf and their family membership at the Loon Lake Country Club. But when Marvin retired from the paper mill and wanted to learn taxidermy, the hammer came down again. She refused to let him buy the equipment and textbooks he would need.

That was one of the few times he managed to outwit her. Several of his colleagues at the mill ordered what he needed and made sure a workspace was cleared in one of the warehouses. For two years, Marvin conjured excuses to slip off for a few hours here and there. Eventually, after he sold a deer mount for $750, Gladys relented and let him set up a taxidermy studio in their basement.

Whatever his frustrations in life with Gladys, Marvin never complained. And he adored their daughter.

"To answer your question, Chief Ferris," said Gladys, "yes, I saw a young man hanging around in front of the condos about five fifteen yesterday. I always walk my little munchkin between five and six so I know exactly what time it was."

"How young a man?" asked Lew. "Teenager? Someone in their twenties? Or thirties? Can you describe his appearance, please?"

"I'd put him about twenty years old. Brown hair, nice haircut. He was wearing jeans—*clean* jeans—and a light blue shirt." Lew took notes as Gladys spoke.

"Shoes?"

"Yes, he wore shoes."

"What kind of shoes? Tennis shoes? Hiking boots? Could you see his shoes?"

"Brown—regular shoes. Like men wear to an office."

"So you must have gotten pretty close to have seen all that."

"Not *real* close but I could certainly see him. He turned to look at me, too, because Polly was barking at him."

"Oh—so you did see his face?"

"Oh yes, I did. Nice looking boy. Square-ish head with dark eyes . . . I think."

"Does that bother you?" asked Osborne who was taking his own notes.

"For heaven's sake, Paul. Why should it?"

"No reason. Just . . . wondering."

During a quiet moment while Lew and Osborne continued to take notes, Gladys tipped her head to one side and stared down at a pattern on the Oriental rug in front of her. The vacant expression on her face surprised Osborne. After observing her for a few seconds, he assumed that maybe she was just thinking, trying to remember.

"Could you identify this young man from a photo?" asked Lew. Gladys looked up, startled. "Very likely. Yes, I'm sure I could."

"Have you ever seen this person before?" asked Lew. "Perhaps he was another resident of the condos?"

"Well, I doubt *that*. I walk there every day and I know who comes and goes."

I'll bet you do, thought Osborne. *Nosy bitch.*

He recalled now an incident one summer when Mallory and Cynthia, the latter home from boarding school, were caught with a bunch of other kids having a beer party in the woods. It was Gladys who put the word out that Mallory had been the ringleader—and that sex and drugs were involved. Her version had Cynthia arriving at the party late—after the rampant bad behavior.

The rumor was vicious enough that Mallory was dropped from the summer tennis team. The truth was that a couple of boys who were close friends of his daughter's had organized the get-together and, yes, there was beer, but that was all.

Though Mallory had confessed to her parents who was involved, Osborne had insisted she take her punishment and never tell on the others. He then called Gladys to say that she and Marvin should find another dentist. That was all he said. He did not add that he wanted nothing to do with her. Ever.

"I'm sure that I—" Gladys started to say when with a yelp the dog leaped across her lap and onto the library table, knocking over the Chinese lamp, which tipped in slow motion toward the floor.

Osborne jumped to his feet and crossed the room in hopes of catching the lamp before it hit but the dog's leg tangled in a silk runner under the lamp, pulling the table over onto the lamp, which, amazingly, did not break. Gladys dropped onto her knees to untangle the dog.

"Oh, golly, Gladys—are you all right?" asked Osborne as he reached behind her to raise the table.

"Don't touch that!" said Gladys.

"But the table is heavy—"

"I'll do it. You leave it alone." The dog ran off and Gladys pushed herself to her feet. She grabbed the table with both hands and gave it a shove up. "There," she said, dusting her hands before setting the runner back on the table. "I exercise at Curves every day and I walk two miles. I don't need your help."

She picked up the lamp and set it back on the table. "Polly does this all the time," she said as she sat back down in the wingchair. "Now, what were you asking?"

"Give me a moment," said Lew, studying the notepad in front of her. While Lew checked over her notes, Osborne saw Gladys strike the odd pose again. Both arms in her lap this time, her hands clasped between her knees, she leaned ever so slightly to one side. Her eyes were focused on the floor and, again, she appeared to have her mind elsewhere.

"Okay, Mrs. Daniels, I have one more question for you," said Lew. Gladys's head jerked. It was as if she had forgotten they were there.

"Does your daughter live here with you?"

"What does that have to do with anything?" said Gladys, her tone hostile.

"Just confirming who travels the road between here and the condo complex on a regular basis," said Lew. "I don't mean to upset you. It's a question we're asking all the people living within two miles of the condo."

"Yes," said Gladys with a huff. "If you must know, she lives in the guest house down near the water. And, you know," Gladys looked off as she spoke, "that poor girl puts in way too many hours. She should never have gone into medicine. I blame her father for encouraging that. She should be married, raising children and keeping a lovely home." Gladys looked like she was about to cry.

Osborne couldn't resist. "Gladys," he said in the tone he used when advising patients to either floss or lose their teeth, "Cynthia works thirty-six hours a week. That is barely full-time and I'm sure she is very well paid."

"Mrs. Daniels," said Lew, breaking in as if worried there might be fireworks, "thank you for your time. I hope to have photos of suspects very soon. When I do, will you mind coming down to the station to see if you recognize the man you saw? Do you drive?"

"Of course I drive," said Gladys, getting to her feet. "Yes, I would be happy to come to the station, just call when you're ready."

"I have a question," said Osborne as he stood up. "What time did Cynthia get home from the clinic yesterday?"

At that Gladys's face turned as livid as her shirt. "My daughter's schedule is none of your business, Paul. Now you stay out of this!" She shook a finger at him. "You never liked Cynthia—just because she is smarter and prettier than that silly daughter of yours. You leave her out of this.

"If you want to . . . to . . . You should be asking about that . . . that awful girl who was killed. That's who you should be asking questions about—not my Cynthia."

"What about that girl?" asked Lew. "Did you know Jennifer Williams?"

"No! I just know about her is all. She was a whore. The entire hospital knows that."

"You mean 'the clinic'?" said Lew in a gentle voice.

"The clinic, the hospital—who the hell cares." Gladys's jowls shook so ferociously Osborne worried she would burst a blood vessel or worse. God forbid he should have to do CPR on the woman.

"I believe we can check with Dr. Daniels on the time of her arrival at home yesterday," said Lew. Her placating tone calmed Gladys.

"Where's my Polly?" Gladys peered around the room, then knelt to look under the chair she had been sitting in.

"We'll show ourselves out, Mrs. Daniels. Thank you for your time."

Chapter Twelve

As Lew turned left off Bobcat Lane and onto the county road, she glanced over at Osborne. He was staring out the passenger-side window, a pained expression on his face.

"Doc, you haven't said a word since getting in the car. Are you okay?"

"Yeah, I'm fine." He didn't sound fine. Lew watched him run a hand through his hair as if the gesture might clear his mind. Crossing his arms, he slouched back against the seat. He looked exhausted.

She checked the rearview mirror. No vehicles in sight. Pulling onto the shoulder and putting the car in park, she said, "What is it? You don't look so good."

Inhaling through gritted teeth, Osborne said, "O-o-h, it's that woman. Being around her brings back so . . . *many* . . . unpleasant memories." He closed his eyes and rubbed his forehead with one hand. "Don't worry. I'll get over it."

Lew studied his face, hoping to see him lighten up a little but the expression on his face remained somber. "Well, if you ask me," she said in a lighthearted tone as she turned toward him, "Gladys Daniels is in dire need of an anger management intervention. Not a class, not a training session—an *intervention*." Osborne didn't smile.

She placed a hand on his knee. "Honestly, Doc, you look like you lost your best friend."

"Did you see the way her body changed? How she got that strange look on her face?" he asked.

"I did. It was like shape-shifting," said Lew. "For a minute I thought she might be having a stroke. Or turning into a werewolf." Lew checked for a shadow of a grin but no luck.

"And her anger when I asked what time Cynthia had arrived home?"

"Now that was not rational," said Lew. "The woman is unstable. No doubt about it."

Turning away from the side window and with a sidelong glance at Lew, Osborne spoke in a voice so low Lew could barely hear him: "Mary Lee behaved like that when she was angry. She would explode. Come at me like an animal. Even her voice changed."

He straightened up and took a deep breath. "She wouldn't make sense. She would be so angry—her whole body would vibrate. Lew, it was like a different person had entered the room. Scared the living hell out of me."

"What would you do?"

"Agree to whatever the issue was. Anything to calm her down. And . . . leave. I'd go fishing." Osborne raised his eyebrows. "Coward's way out, I know."

"Doc, did she ever behave that way *before* you were married?"

"Are you kidding? If she had, I would have been out of there so fast . . . No, Mary Lee managed to keep her bad behaviors in check until after the girls were born. That's when all hell broke loose."

"Did she ever hit you?"

Osborne was quiet for a moment. "She didn't hit *me*, but once when we were still living in town she threw a heavy wooden rocking chair through the big plate glass window in our living room. That took strength. I'm not sure I could have done it."

"What about your daughters? Did she get that angry with them?"

"Not that I am aware of. But I have to say I've been afraid to ask." Osborne mulled over the question. "If she did, I think Erin would have told me. She was never her mother's favorite. I used to worry that she might hurt the girls—physically or emotionally— but they seemed okay."

Before Lew could offer words of assurance, Osborne asked, "Where does uncontrolled anger like that come from? You must see it in law enforcement. . . ."

"We do. But there's no predicting the source. I know what you're talking about, Doc. My ex would let things simmer, then fly into a rage. Especially after drinking. In his case, it was a family tradition. I should've seen it coming.

"Doc," Lew nudged his shoulder, "you can't blame yourself for Mary Lee's actions. You're a big boy, you know that."

Osborne managed a sheepish look, "Well . . . I feel better having talked about it. It's just . . . that outburst from Gladys made me feel like I was locked in a room with Mary Lee all over again." He shook his head in sadness.

Lew reached for his chin and tipped his face toward hers, "For the record? I find you to be a good man. A *kind* man. Pretty special in my world."

"Thanks," said Osborne, his voice soft.

"And there is no percentage in letting the past haunt you. Right?"

"Right."

Lew put the squad car in gear. Listening to Osborne, she'd felt a wave of tenderness for this gentle man who had been as bruised in the heart as victims whose bodies carried signs of physical abuse.

More than once it had occurred to her that if Osborne's mother had not died when he was six—leaving him with a father who never remarried and sent his young son off to boarding school—that if he had known what a good marriage could be that he might have avoided Mary Lee.

Might have. On the other hand, you can't cheat destiny.

They drove through Loon Lake in silence. A few blocks from the police station, Lew spoke up, "Frankly, Doc, even though it was hard on you, I see a plus to what just happened. It's obvious that

Gladys Daniels is disturbed. That calls into question her supposed sighting of the man she alleges to have killed Jennifer Williams."

"You don't believe her?"

"I'm beginning to wonder if she made the whole thing up. Now I know I've told you this before, but I learned a long time ago that the worst witness is an eyewitness. And did you hear the venom in her voice when she talked about Jennifer Williams?"

"Yes," said Osborne. "That was a surprise."

"Certainly was. I intend to question her more on *that* subject. You don't have to be there if you don't want to, Doc."

"I'll be fine," said Osborne as she pulled into the police station parking lot and stopped near his car, "although I have one question for you."

"What's that?"

"You won't forget I've invited you for dinner and an hour in the boat this evening? I'd like to try that 'suspended musky' technique you've been telling me about. Might take the kids along, too."

"The *kids?*"

"Beth has a friend from basketball camp she's invited for dinner— a boy."

"Ha!" said Lew. "Am I brilliant or what? Told ya." She grinned. "Sure, I'd love to join you later, but it's already four o'clock. I may not be able to get to your place until six thirty or seven. Is that too late?"

"You bring the bait, I got the boat."

As Osborne stepped out of the car, Lew leaned forward to say, "One more reason I doubt that old woman. Does it not occur to her that if she really did see someone and someone who knows she could identify him—that *she* might be in jeopardy? You have to be fairly close to a person to notice they have a 'nice haircut.' So why isn't she concerned for her own safety?"

Lew shook her head, "The more I think about that wacky old woman—she wasted our time."

"You're probably right," said Osborne.

As he climbed into his car, he made a mental note to call his oldest daughter later. Be interesting to hear what she would have to say about Gladys Daniels, the woman who had done her evil best to ruin Mallory's reputation.

Chapter Thirteen

As Lew hurried into the police station, she spotted a tall, scrawny kid in dirty jeans and a rumpled black T-shirt seated on a bench across from the switchboard. He jumped to his feet as she approached and rushed toward her. Lew stopped short, taken aback to see he was wearing earmuffs under a filthy white baseball cap he'd crammed onto his head—a nutty thing to do on such a hot day.

Was he one of the patients from the mental health center who sometimes drifted into the station convinced the CIA was tapping their phones? But as the kid closed in, Lew got a better look at the earmuffs and relaxed when she saw they were clumps of frizzy hair camouflaging his ears.

"Chief Ferris?" The boy's voice, high and tense, wavered as he spoke. "I'm the guy with the pickup got stole. Please, you gotta help me. If I don't have it by tomorrow morning, I'm gonna lose my job." He was so upset, he was shaking.

"Okay, okay, young man," said Lew, motioning for him to back off a few feet. "I know about the problem with your truck. Let me check with the supervisor here and see if we've made any progress locating it."

The kid made no move to get out of her way. "I gotta get the truck!"

"I heard you. Now," said Lew, pointing to the bench and hardening her voice, "sit . . . down." He sat.

Lew walked over to the glass partition that separated the switchboard from the main entrance and waiting area. To her surprise, the department's veteran operator was nowhere in sight.

"Dani?" she asked the young intern as she pressed the button that let her into the glass-enclosed space housing the switchboard, "where is Marlaine?"

"Oh, hi Chief Ferris," said Dani, grinning up at Lew from where she sat in the operator's chair, "Marlaine left to help her daughter run one of the grandkids to the emergency room. He fell off his bike and may have fractured his skull. So I took over." Lew couldn't help noticing that Dani had maneuvered the operator headset into position on her burst of curls so that it looked like she was wearing an electronic tiara.

While Dani knew computers—and hair and makeup—Lew had no confidence in her skills on the police switchboard: radio communication, walkie-talkies, cell phones, smart phones, and 911 calls required serious skills and awareness of legal protocols. Not to mention the ability to determine whether a call from a citizen was an emergency or a prank.

"Ah . . . Dani?" asked Lew, not sure how to approach the issue without hurting the young woman's feelings, "sure you know how to handle the calls?" Before Dani could answer, Lew checked her watch. "I'll see if Robin can't come in early to hold down the fort." Robin was Marlaine's niece and the night operator. She was experienced.

Standing with her back to the waiting area, Lew jerked a thumb in the direction of the kid with the stolen truck: "Any news on that?"

Dani shook her head. "Not that I know of. Only that he's sure some guy named Alvin Marski stole it. That's on Marlaine's note here." Dani pointed to a legal pad with Marlaine's scribbles on it. Lew picked up the legal pad to see what else Marlaine had flagged.

"One call you should be aware of, Chief," said Dani, speaking as if she was the teacher and Lew the student. "There was a break-in out on Squirrel Lake. Roger said he would look into it. He's out there now."

"What's the address?" asked Lew.

"Um, um, let me check my notes. . . . Oh, here it is—the James McNeil residence. Someone broke into their basement—"

"McNeil?" said Lew, backing toward the door. "You should have alerted me right away."

"Oh, but—Marlaine said not to call you unless it was something important. Oh, dear, I did the wrong thing?" Dani's eyes filled with anxiety.

"Dani," said Lew, keeping her voice level even as she wanted to speak fast, "breaking and entering is a felony. Please, radio Roger right now and tell him I am on my way and he is to stop whatever he is doing and wait for my arrival."

She didn't add that Roger's competency as a deputy started and ended with emptying parking meters. Having chosen law enforcement as a second career when he found selling insurance too much effort, Roger's ineptitude in filling out a police report had given Lew enough nightmares. She did not need another, and especially if it concerned someone with a connection to an unsolved murder.

"Dani—why did you not think this was serious?"

"Because they said it happened a while ago, like yesterday or the day before. Chief?"

"What?" Lew tried hard not to be short with the girl.

"There is another call. . . ."

"Okay, what's that?"

"Um, the crime lab guy—"

"Bruce Peters?"

"Right. He called and asked for Ray Pradt—said he needs help tracking, so I gave him Mr. Pradt's phone number." Lew's shoulders sagged. "I did the wrong thing, huh?"

"Oh," said Lew shaking her head in frustration. "Here's the way it has to work, Dani. Wait, please, don't cry. You didn't know and now you're learning, and we can work this out. But Ray Pradt is not a police officer. Far from it."

Lew stopped there, choosing not to mention the Loon Lake Police Department's file on Ray Pradt—the one bulging with a history of misdemeanors for indulging in a type of grass not grown in Kentucky, poaching giant trout from private ponds, and, at age eight, being the Loon Lake vendor of record for illegal fireworks. Ray never let the law get in the way of his vision of entrepreneurship.

Though his father had been a prominent physician, his older brother a hand surgeon, and his sister a well-known trial lawyer in Chicago, Ray was less concerned with degrees, money, and consumer goods.

He lived in a trailer home painted to resemble a humongous muskie, drove a battered truck with a leaping walleye for a hood ornament, and dedicated his days to spending as much time in the outdoors as weather would allow.

To his credit, he was the only person Lew had ever known who could get a deer to eat out of his hand. And he was an expert tracker, which was a talent both the Loon Lake Police and the Wausau Crime Lab had utilized more than once.

Lew suspected that Bruce Peters had been brusque in demanding that Dani reach Ray "ASAP"—a request that Marlaine would have known to run by Lew. Nor would Marlaine have been intimidated by gruff, good-looking, nerdy Bruce.

"Dani, department policy requires that Ray Pradt be deputized by me before he is allowed to work on an investigation. And I need to check my budget before I hire him."

"But Bruce said—"

"I don't care what Bruce said. He's not in charge."

"He said," Dani gulped her words out between sobs, "he said it might rain tonight so Ray had to get to those condos where they found that woman right away. That's what he said so—"

"Dani, take it easy. I'm just letting you know what the procedures are around here. Now, please, I'm running out to the McNeils, I have my cell phone and the radio is always on in the cruiser. Any emergencies of any kind—notify me right away. I'll reach Robin and ask her to relieve you."

"Chief Ferris," Dani wiped at her cheeks, "I am so sorry."

"Later," said Lew. "You're not fired, so relax. I know you were doing your best." Back at the bench where the owner of the stolen truck was sitting in dutiful silence, Lew handed him her notepad and said, "Write down your name and phone number. I have an emergency but I will put one of my deputies on this right away and see if he can locate any new information on your truck."

As Lew pushed open the door to leave the station, Dani ran up to hand her a note. "Sorry, Chief, I almost forgot this and he asked me to be sure you get this today." Glancing down, Lew saw that the mayor wanted a morning meeting. Great, she thought, a budget hearing now? Maybe she could persuade him to hold off a few days.

Moments later she was on the road to the McNeils, siren blaring, lights flashing.

Chapter Fourteen

Lew pulled up behind Roger's squad car just as a dark green convertible zoomed by only to brake hard at the front door of the two-story contemporary lake home belonging to the McNeils. Leaping from the driver's seat, Jim McNeil slammed his car door shut and half-walked, half-ran toward Lew. He was not smiling.

"Mr. McNeil, I thought you would have been here half an hour ago," said Lew, eyes full of surprise. "That's when my officer arrived. About then anyway."

"Chief Ferris, we need to talk," said McNeil through gritted teeth as he thrust his hands deep into his pockets. Rocking back and forth on his heels, he said, "This is at least the *fourth* time my wife has called me insisting there is a prowler. Not once have I seen any evidence that there is, in fact, a prowler. Raccoons, yes, deer, yes, people, no.

"And I am embarrassed to say this but . . ." He dropped his head and, glancing off to one side, bit his lower lip as if struggling with what he might say. Making up his mind, he took a deep breath and said, "My dear wife, Leigh, is so paranoid these days that I am convinced—especially after today—that she needs professional help. Her imagination is out of control. Chief Ferris, she has worked herself into a state of hysteria."

Looking over McNeil's shoulder as he spoke, Lew spotted Roger waving to her from a doorway beside the attached garage. "Down in the basement, Chief," shouted Roger. "This way."

McNeil spun around.

"Let's discuss your wife and the calls once I get a handle on what's going on here," said Lew. She raised a questioning eyebrow toward McNeil. "Sounds like the officer thinks he's found something."

McNeil raised his hands in a gesture of helplessness but followed Lew through the doorway to the stairwell leading down to the basement.

McNeil at her heels, Lew skipped down the basement stairs and followed Roger through a cavernous outer area holding a furnace and storage shelving to a small laundry room where a washer and dryer were situated under two horizontal windows.

Across from the appliances stood an ironing board and iron along with a white Formica-topped kitchen table holding a sewing machine and an assortment of empty wooden frames. A quilt rack holding a partially completed quilt stood nearby along with a smaller table heaped with wrapping papers and baskets of ribbons. It was a pristine, well-organized workroom with southern light streaming in from the overhead windows.

Roger pointed to the dryer, and Lew walked over. At first glance, she thought someone had spilled coffee grounds on top of the appliance. It took a second before her eyes registered that the mess was mud. Examining the muddy patch up close, Lew made out one well-defined print from a shoe and a smear of caked dirt where another shoe might have slid across the top of the dryer. Clumps of dried dirt littered the floor in front of the dryer.

"Check out that window on the right, Chief," said Roger pointing up. Though it hadn't been obvious when she walked into the laundry room, Lew saw that the window, a casement-type that opened out, had been shattered. Only a few shards of glass remained in the frame. "A lotta glass on the floor behind the washer and dryer," said Roger. "I was thinking we might get prints off some of that, Chief. The light in here's not so good right now but earlier I thought I could see a little blood—"

Lew peered around one side of the dryer. Broken glass littered the floor. One shard did have a dark stain running across it. She looked up at the broken window. "My guess is the intruder may have bumped that window accidentally and got cut. Now, Roger, you haven't touched anything in here, right?"

"Umm, not down here," said Roger, his voice hesitant. "I, um, the lady of the house has been pretty upset since I arrived. Been trying to calm her down, see if she can tell us when this might have happened. Had to touch her to help her up the stairs. On the elbow, her left elbow. Hope that's okay?" Roger looked ready to duck.

"Of course that's okay," said Lew. How could a guy be so dumb? She reminded herself to check again to see if she couldn't get him transferred over to the county sheriff. He'd see it as a promotion but for Lew—a relief.

"Any sign of someone attempting to enter the house elsewhere?" asked Lew, reaching for her cell phone.

Roger straightened up, shoulders back with pride. "No, Chief. I checked real careful just before you got here. There's a flower garden outside those windows, and Mrs. McNeil said she had sprinklers going all day yesterday. I found muddy footprints right by this broken window but nowhere else. So we know the source of the mud and the point of entry. That'll help, won't it?"

Lew knew he expected a pat on the head, but she didn't have time. Standing in the doorway behind Roger was McNeil, his eyes moving up to the window and down to the muddied dryer as if trying to comprehend what might have happened.

"When was the last time you were in this room?" Lew asked McNeil.

"Me? I never come down here. This is Leigh's workroom. Good God, I can't believe this," he said, shaking his head in disbelief. "Leigh was right—someone *did* break in. Dammit! What do we do now?"

"I'd check my security system for starters," said Lew, "meanwhile excuse me while I get in touch with one of the techs from the Wausau Crime Lab who's in town working the crime scene over at the condos. If he's got the time, I'd sure like to get him out here tonight.

"Dani," said Lew, turning away from McNeil as she pressed the cell phone to one ear. "Patch me through to Bruce Peters, please. Do you know how to do that? Good." Lew waited, "Bruce? Chief Ferris here. I got a residential break-in with one good impression of the sole of a shoe—looks like a sneaker or a sandal. Also I may have blood and prints on the window they broke getting in."

Lew turned to McNeil, "He's wondering what kind of security system you have—cameras?"

McNeil shook his head. "We got the signs but no activated system. Didn't think we needed one in Loon Lake."

Lew repeated the first part of his answer then said, "Would you and Ray have time this evening to check these out when you're finished there? I'll have Dani give you directions. . . . Great. Ray is still with you, right? Put him on please."

Lew waited as the phone changed hands then said, "Ray, thanks for getting over there so fast, and even though Dani didn't follow protocol, don't worry. You are officially deputized on the project and—" Before she could say more, Ray must have interrupted her because she said, "What?" in an astonished voice. "Say that again."

As Lew listened, Roger and McNeil waited, watching in silence as she said, "Really? You've located a vehicle, too? A pickup? Any registration in it?"

Lew nodded as she listened. "Hmm. Be careful now—don't jump to conclusions. Just because it's parked so close to the condos doesn't mean the driver killed Jennifer Williams. If it's as beat up as you say, could have been junked by someone.

"Hold on for a minute and let me check my notes." Lew handed her cell phone to Roger and, reaching for her notepad, she opened it to where she had written down the name of the kid whose truck was missing. Taking back her phone, she said, "Yeah, it's the same guy," she said. "This could be a simple coincidence but tell Bruce to impound the vehicle so he can check for prints and DNA.

"Now, Ray, I have a break-in out at Squirrel Lake. . . ." After describing the scene in the McNeils' basement, Lew said, "So I told Bruce what I need here from him, but I want you to get a good shot, black and white and color, of this footprint on the dryer. Then see what you can find outside—any indication of how the individual got access to the property."

Before putting her phone away, Lew checked back in with Dani: "Bruce and Ray have located the pickup that was stolen from that kid. I need you to make two calls. First, call the Honda dealer over on Highway 51 and arrange for that young man to rent one of their used vehicles. Our department has an account with them—just use my name.

"Then call the owner of the pickup and tell him we need to run some tests on his vehicle. He can pick up a rental and the Loon Lake Police Department will cover the cost. Absolutely do not say anything more than that. I don't need anyone jumping to conclusions.

"Oh, one more thing. Ask the owner to stop by the station because Bruce will need his prints in order to sort out what he might find in the truck. Remember how to take a person's fingerprints? Good. Last thing—I did reach Robin and she'll be in to relieve you at six. And, Dani—thank you."

Putting her phone away, Lew turned to Roger. "I want you to hustle back to the station and check the files. I need all the information you can get on Alvin Marski—where he's living, where he's working, where he is at this moment. See what you can find out and let me know ASAP. And, Roger, alert Todd that I may need backup during an arrest shortly. His shift doesn't start until eight so you may have to reach him at home."

"Holy cow," said Roger. "You think Marski killed that girl?"

"I don't know what to think—and you don't either. All we know for sure is that Alvin borrowed that truck a couple days ago and hasn't returned it.

"What Ray said was he was able to follow a set of tracks from the site where the body was found—apparently the killer got some blood on his shoes. But Ray lost the trail for several hundred yards. By chance, he spotted a vehicle parked on the bike path that runs behind the clinic and those condos.

"That does not mean the two are connected. Knowing Alvin Marski, he probably ran out of gas, ran out of cash, and walked off."

Lew looked over at McNeil, "We're discussing an individual who is a repeat offender, a small-time crook—stealing fishing equipment and gas cans from pontoon boats. I'm going to be very surprised if there is any connection between Alvin Marski and Jennifer Williams.

"So my point, Roger, is that even if you have heard me say that Marski is a person of interest, don't assume he's done anything more than run off with a buddy's pickup."

As Lew motioned for the two men to follow her upstairs, she said, "Mr. McNeil, I will need you and your wife to stay out of the basement and your yard until Bruce and Ray have looked everything over."

"Fine," said McNeil with a wave of his hands.

"Whew," said Lew after Roger had driven off. "This has been one busy afternoon. Mr. McNeil, let's go see your wife."

"Come on," said McNeil with a sheepish and attractive grin, "I wish you would call me Jim."

"Okay . . . Jim." Lew managed a half-smile. "But before we talk to your wife—does that name, Alvin Marski, sound familiar? He wouldn't be someone who has been employed at the clinic? Food service? Maintenance?"

"Not that I'm aware," said McNeil. "I'm happy to call our HR person just to be sure."

"I would appreciate that," said Lew.

Before following McNeil into his kitchen where Leigh was waiting with a drink in her hand, Lew took a moment to make one last call. She got Osborne's voice mail.

"Doc, please save me something for dinner but go ahead without me. If you're still up for it and I get there before nine, let's plan to fish even if it's only for an hour.

"Let me rephrase that: I *need* time on the water."

Chapter Fifteen

Lew could see that once upon a time McNeil's wife had been stunning. White-blond hair pulled smooth, twisted into a chignon at the base of her neck, and married to a creamy complexion and wide Delft-blue eyes gave her a doll-like prettiness. But prettiness marred by too much flesh.

Whatever the cause—an excess of food or drink, lack of exercise, or too many meds—the woman's delicate bone structure was hidden beneath jowls, puffy rings around the eyes, and cheeks that swung too loose. No doubt the redness in her face was due to the emotions of the moment, but Lew sensed this was a woman who never woke feeling happy.

"I am terrified," said Leigh, pounding a fist on the table as she sat in a kitchen chair across from Lew and her husband. The small tape recorder Lew had placed in the center of the table bounced and flipped over. As Lew turned it right side up, Leigh picked up a yellow legal pad in front of her and shook it in the direction of McNeil.

"Jim, we have got to move out until the police find the person who's stalking me. I am so totally frightened I cannot sleep here another night."

"Leigh . . ." said her husband, a note of caution hanging in the air, "we are not doing that. I'm calling the security firm and we'll get the system repaired and upgraded. Again."

He turned to Lew, "The security system built into this house keeps blowing during electrical storms. Vibrations set it off so easily that half the time I don't use it."

"Worse than that," said Leigh. "Whoever is stalking us does something remotely to turn it off. Remember? Last week when you were at the conference in Appleton, it went out. The weather was fine."

McNeil raised his hands in a gesture of futility. "I don't know," he said to Lew. "I've had the security guys out here at least five times in the last few months. They can't find anything wrong except the electrical storm issue, which happens to everyone in the area. We're waiting on a new base unit so the system has been off for the last week."

"I want cameras," said Leigh, whining like a six-year-old.

"Cameras will cost us thousands of dollars," said McNeil. "That's overkill, and I've told you that."

Leigh glared. "After what happened today?"

"All right. I'll look into it."

Before the two could argue further, Lew jumped in to change the subject. "Is there anyone that either of you know who might be aware that your system has been off?" she asked. Leigh and her husband both shook their heads. "Anyone at your office?"

"Not that I can think of," said McNeil with another shake of his head.

"Look, Leigh," he said in a conciliatory tone, "I'm sure I can get someone out here tomorrow, and I'm home for the next ten days. That security firm runs the systems for the clinic. They know who I am, that I approve their invoices, and you can bet they will bend over backward to get this taken care of. Okay?"

Staring at the notepad in front of her, Leigh managed a whisper: "Okay."

"Mrs. McNeil," said Lew, "I have some questions for you."

"Richards," said Leigh. "Leigh Richards. I've never changed my name. When Jim and I got married, I was a vice president for a brokerage firm in Madison and it didn't make sense to put all my clients through a name change."

"I see," said Lew. "You work from home now?"

"Not since Jim went into management," said Leigh. "I haven't worked in over six years."

"Ah," said Lew as she jotted a note while thinking: Nothing worse than a bright, bored, and lonely housewife. "Before we discuss that list in front of you, can you give me an idea when you were last in that downstairs workroom?"

"Yesterday. I worked on my quilt all morning," said Leigh. "I do every stitch by hand."

"One of her quilts is hanging in the state capitol building down in Madison," said McNeil with pride.

"Nice," said Lew. "And this morning? You were working down there until what time?"

"No. Today I saw the dermatologist. I didn't go downstairs until three o'clock or so. That's when I saw the mess and . . ." She inhaled harshly and tried to speak but waved one hand as she choked.

"Take your time," said Lew.

"Umm," Leigh pushed a Kleenex against her eyes. "Whoever broke in took four squares of the quilt that I was working on. I've been working on them for weeks and had laid them on the ironing board and . . . they're gone." She took a deep breath and turned her shoulders away from her husband.

"Jim doesn't believe me but that's the kind of thing that's been happening. Whoever it is—is after me. Not Jim—me. I know it sounds like I'm making all this up." She raised sad eyes to Lew, "I can't prove I had my quilt squares there, but I did. I know I did." A soft sob into the Kleenex.

"When you're ready," said Lew, tapping her pen, "I want to hear about all the other times you've been convinced someone was here."

After blowing her nose and wiping at her eyes, Leigh pulled the legal pad closer to her. "Okay," she said, sniffling, "I've made a list. It started last November when Jim was away at a conference in Hawaii. I was watching television one night in the den when I happened to look up and see this awful face in the window. Just for a second then it was gone—but I know I saw someone."

"A man or a woman?"

"I don't know. They wore a black mask with bleeding eyes. Jim thought it was kids playing a prank after Halloween."

"Have you seen the face since?"

"No. But I have seen movement at different windows. Like I'll look over and get just a glimpse of something or someone. That's why I want security cameras. All we have is a system that works if a window or door is opened or if there is a vibration from someone trying to enter. We can't see around the outside of the house if someone is lurking. . . ."

"And does this always happen after dark?"

"Yes, and always when Jim is not home. So the first time it happened was in November. Then, just before Christmas, I went out to my car one night and someone had been in it.

"They had taken one of my favorite cookbooks from the kitchen here," Leigh pointed over to a shelf holding a dozen or more cookbooks, "cut it up into little tiny pieces and dumped it into the back of my Jeep. Jim thought I had forgotten a book back there and it got wet and shredded—but I know I didn't."

"Cut not torn?"

"Cut. With scissors. The pieces were less than a quarter inch," said Leigh, holding up two fingers to demonstrate. "That took time. And what a nutty thing to do. I know this sounds crazy but I got the message: they wanted to use the scissors on me."

"Cut you up?"

"Or cut me out."

That's interesting, thought Lew. Darn, she wished Doc were there to listen in on this. She would make sure he listened to the tape.

"In February, Jim was traveling, and when I went to take the trash out for pickup the next morning, the door to the garage was open and the motion sensor lights over the driveway had been turned off. I did not turn those off, and they were on just fine after Jim left that week."

She took a deep breath. "I cannot tell you how many times I find doors left open that I know I closed—the garage door, the door to the garden shed, the door to the boathouse.

"But the worst is what happened to my garden and my boat."

Lew checked her watch. She hoped Bruce and Ray would show up before she finished talking with Leigh.

"In June, I put in a new bed of daylilies—wonderful varieties I found over in Minneapolis and a very expensive Japanese maple. Destroyed. I woke up one morning and someone had pulled the daylilies right out of the ground and cut off my little tree."

"Deer," muttered Jim McNeil.

"Jim," said Leigh with a tinge of hysteria in her voice, "I put fencing around those. Deer can't yank up fencing." McNeil rolled his eyes and shrugged.

"I'll want you to show my deputy, Ray Pradt, and Bruce Peters from the Wausau Crime Lab where that happened," said Lew. "They should be here any minute, I hope."

Lew could understand why McNeil found it difficult to believe his wife. Every thing she had described so far could be blamed on wind, weather, or critters, including raccoons, rabbits, foxes, deer, bears, and coyotes—pests familiar to anyone living in the North-woods. Her own garden fell victim to prairie dogs so often she kept a sixteen-gauge shotgun by the kitchen door.

As far as the mask in the window—could have been a raccoon, especially if Leigh enjoyed an evening cocktail or two. But the cut-up book. Now that was weird.

"A deer did not desecrate my boat," said Leigh, glaring at her husband. She turned to Lew saying, "That happened two weeks ago and it's when I called nine-one-one.

"Someone broke into our boathouse and left a disgusting pile of dog poop in my rowboat. It's an antique I inherited from my grandfather—a lovely little wooden rowboat. It's painted green on the outside and beautifully varnished inside and out. Or it was until someone put the dog poop in it, which ate through the varnish and left an ugly stain. Of course, Jim thought it was a raccoon."

McNeil caught Lew's eye and nodded.

"What made you think it was *dog* poop and not left by another animal?" asked Lew.

"My mother had a Yorkie and it looked just like that dog's poop. I'm not stupid—I know dog poop from deer scat and rabbit droppings—I garden, I know what animals do.

"Plus, *plus*," said Leigh waving one finger to emphasize her point, "the damn boat is suspended from the roof of the boathouse and over the water—so how does an animal get in and out without drowning?" She sat back satisfied she had made a key point.

"So what we do know," said Lew, looking down at her notes, "is that the break-in downstairs has to have occurred sometime yesterday afternoon or evening. But maybe this morning. Is that correct?"

"Yes," said Leigh.

"Aside from the face in the window that night, have you seen anyone else on your property?"

"Well . . . no," said Leigh. "And again I know this sounds like I'm nuts, but even though I don't *see* anyone—I get the feeling I'm being watched. Last spring I stopped doing any quilting at night because I sensed someone was peering in the basement window."

"But you didn't call nine-one-one then?"

Before she could answer, her husband interrupted in a stern voice, "Leigh, I want you to tell Chief Ferris about your medications."

She threw him a look so angry, Lew wondered how long this marriage was going to last. "I've been on antidepressants. Not LSD or crack cocaine. Antidepressants. And so what?" She threw her hands up. "Half the women I know are on antidepressants. I am not hallucinating."

A knock at the kitchen door prompted Lew to turn around. "Oh, good. That's probably my team," she said as Jim McNeil rose from his chair.

Chapter Sixteen

Leaving Bruce and Ray to pick their way through the broken glass and muddy prints left in the laundry room, Lew followed Leigh down to the boathouse, a small building that must have been built years ago, as it rested on timbers allowing it to hover over the water.

"Aren't *you* lucky to have an old boathouse like this," said Lew, amazed to discover one of the antique structures that once dotted Northwoods' shorelines but have since been outlawed.

"I know people aren't allowed to build so close to water these days, so we were fortunate to find this place," said Leigh.

"It's wonderful the way you've restored the boathouse," said Lew, admiring the small structure with its fresh coat of dark green paint. Crisp white trim outlined the windows, which appeared to contain their original glass from the early 1900s. An upper level hinted of an old-fashioned sleeping porch.

"You know," said Lew with a shake of her head, "I understand the DNR's reasoning for their shoreline restrictions but I do miss the old places. My uncle had a boathouse like this, and when I was a kid, I loved the upstairs sleeping porch—listening to the lake all night long." Lew smiled.

"I know what you mean," said Leigh. "The boathouse is why we bought the property. It's all that was left from the original buildings on the land. Thank goodness the developer was smart enough to leave it. It's grandfathered in, so we were able to restore a certain amount— we painted the exterior and replaced some of the wooden decking."

She opened the door and they stepped into a dark interior. Two boats and a jet ski were moored inside. Lew walked past a small cabin cruiser to where a petite rowboat, so old it was likely made by hand in the early 1900s, hung suspended shoulder height over open water. The weathered varnish on the exterior gleamed even in the dim light and the oars boasted silver fittings that would be impossible to find today.

"Where did you find this rowboat?" asked Lew. "It's beautiful."

"My grandfather made it. He was a doctor by profession and carpentry was his hobby." Leigh lowered the pulley that was holding the boat down far enough that they had a view of the interior.

"Oh, oh, I see what you mean," said Lew, peering into the small craft. Whatever the mess made by a critter, the result was a dark stain marring the warm brown finish.

"Chief Ferris, if you look up," said Leigh, pointing at the cables holding the boat, "you can see that when this boat is raised it has to be impossible for an animal to climb up, over, and into the boat—not without help."

"You would be surprised," said Lew. "Your boathouse has plenty of room beneath those lakeside doors. An eagle or other predator could find their way in and drop a dead fish or some other small animal in here. Unless you're a forensic expert, it can be difficult to tell the smell of decomposing—"

"I know the smell of dog shit."

Lew shrugged. The woman had made up her mind. She walked over to the speedboat, which sat on an elaborate electric shore station. "No damage to this craft?" she asked as she examined the interior of the speedboat. "Have you checked the interior of that cabin for signs of a break-in or damage?"

"Nothing. The only damage was to my boat. That one is Jim's pride and joy." A note of resentment had crept into Leigh's voice.

"Quite the setup, you have here," said Lew. "I don't see many shore stations this fancy. All you have to do is flip that switch and the shore station automatically raises or lowers the boat, right?"

"My husband's a gear head. Anything you can power up, he has to have. Boats, cars, a motorcycle. Hard to get him to just stay home and take life easy." Leigh sighed.

Lew smiled in understanding. An aura of sadness around the woman gave her the urge to do or say something that might make her feel better.

"You know, Leigh," said Lew after a long pause during which she studied the rowboat and the stain on the floor of the little craft, "I could be wrong about your rowboat. Even though I have seen animals accomplish amazing feats, I'll ask one of the deputies you just met to check this out, too.

"Ray Pradt is an expert on animal behavior—and he has two dogs of his own. Big dogs. Yellow Labs. If anyone knows the damage dog excrement can do, it'll be Ray. That aside, he's a skilled tracker who insists he can tell the size and age of an animal from its scat. You didn't happen to keep a sample of what you found in the boat, did you?"

"Sorry," said Leigh. "I couldn't get rid of it fast enough. Is Ray the taller of those two guys? The real good-looking one?"

"Yep, that's Ray," said Lew with a grin. Turning away from Leigh, she rolled her eyes: Ray and women. Some things never change.

As they left the boathouse, Lew spotted Ray and Bruce up on the patio, both men on their knees near the broken window.

"Ray? Bruce?" At the sound of her voice they got to their feet and turned toward her.

The two men could not appear less likely to be a working pair.

Ray was a rangy six feet five inches tall and very tan with bare knees exposed beneath a pair of wrinkled khaki shorts. He wore a baggy white T-shirt with the words "Severe Fishing Disorder" stenciled in black and readable from miles away.

His hair—in grave need of a trim and hostage to the August humidity—was an explosion of dark brown ringlets capable of hiding a covey of grouse. A thirty-two-year-old stuck in his teens.

The other guy, Bruce Peters of the Wausau Crime Lab, appeared the consummate professional in pressed gray Dockers and a muted green and tan checked shirt. A disciplined crew cut and a matching black mustache completed the picture.

But while Bruce had proved to be an experienced, diligent forensic scientist, Lew knew from experience that he shared a few too many characteristics with Ray: a love for the outdoors and fishing—and an irreverent sense of humor. Kids at heart, those two.

Granted she had criminal cases to solve—cases that benefited from their skills—Lew was well aware her real challenge was managing those two razzbonyas.

"Chief," said Bruce, dusting his hands as he walked up, "we've bagged shards of glass and other evidence that may be helpful. I will arrange for DNA testing on the bloodstains and run the results against our state and national databases but it may take a week or more."

"I figured as much," said Lew, "are you driving back to Wausau tonight?"

Bruce threw a glance at Ray and Lew detected a smothered grin. "Oh, no," said Bruce, his eyes so serious she knew something was up. "I'm going to camp out here over the weekend. That stolen pickup will take some work, then I need to search the home and office of your victim. I'd like to be here when the pathologist report comes in, too. Never know what might be needed."

"Bruce, my budget—" Lew started to protest.

"He can stay at my place," said Ray. "No charge."

"That's dangerous," said Lew. She gave Bruce the dim eye. "Are you sure?"

But bushy eyebrows bounced happily as Bruce said, "Oh yeah. I'm gonna check out Ray's new fishing kayak while I'm here. And, Chief, I won't charge overtime for my work on Saturday and Sunday. . . ."

Lew gave a cautious nod. "All right, then. But right now let's talk about the situation here." The two men glanced at each other, pleased. Shoulders back, they prepared to listen.

"Mr. McNeil and his wife are quite concerned that the intruder may return. They think the individual has trespassed here on several occasions previously." Lew detailed the instances that Leigh had described earlier. "Ray, did you find any sign of where or how they may have approached the property—recently or earlier?"

"Nope," said Ray. "There was a lawn crew here this morning and with no rain the last few days—not much for me to work with."

"I see," said Lew. "Several weeks ago someone may have broken into their boathouse, too."

Lew turned to Leigh who was standing nearby. "Tell Ray your concern over the rowboat, would you?"

Leigh perked up and described in detail her theory that someone had deliberately allowed a dog to desecrate her precious antique boat.

"So if you two would check out the boathouse before you leave here this evening," said Lew, "that would be helpful. Oh, and one more thought, Ray—what are you doing with those webcams of yours?"

"Nothing, why?"

"The security system here is being upgraded but they won't have security cameras in place for a while. How difficult would it be for you to rig your webcams so Jim and Leigh can see the exterior of their house from indoors?"

"Wait a minute," said McNeil who had walked onto the patio moments earlier and heard Lew's question. "How much is this going to cost me?"

"Jim—" said Leigh, turning a threatening eye on her husband.

"Eh," said Ray with a shrug, "I'm not using the darn things until deer season. Takes five minutes to set the cameras up, and the monitor is wireless. All you do is turn it on and you get a split screen with views from both cameras. Records great in low light by the way. I use it to check nocturnal visitors to my deer stand."

"Like bears?" said Leigh with a shiver of delight. Lew couldn't believe how the woman had perked up.

"Bears, fishers, fox, 'coons, porcupines—all my buddies," said Ray. "Better 'n *Letterman* some nights.

"I have the whole shebang set to record a forty-eight-hour loop, then erase and start over. You can watch in real time or fast-forward whenever you want. Fifty bucks sound okay to you?"

"Yes," said Leigh, not waiting for a response from her husband. "But how soon can you set it up?"

"After Bruce and I finish here, I'll drive back to my place and get all the parts. Should be able to set it up tonight. Be good to test the video in the dark—make sure you can see everything okay."

"Ohmygosh, that is just great," said Leigh with so much enthusiasm that even Ray was taken aback. Only McNeil had a skeptical expression on his face.

"Did you say you hunt deer?" asked Leigh.

Ray looked around at Bruce and Lew: "Is this northern Wisconsin?"

"I have a question for you then," said Leigh. "When I was twelve my grandfather taught me how to shoot a twenty-two-caliber pistol but I haven't shot a gun since. Jim keeps a shotgun in the house but I've never shot one. I think I'd feel better if I knew how to handle that gun."

Oh dear, thought Lew.

"I'll take you to the shooting range if you'd like," said Ray.

"I would *love* that."

Back in her squad car, Lew radioed in to the station. "Todd," she said on reaching the night deputy on duty, "I'm on my way in and I'd like you to help me bring Alvin Marski in for questioning on that stolen pickup and—"

Todd interrupted before she could finish. "Chief, I made a few calls. Roger told me you were hoping to do this but it's not going to be all that easy. Alvin's mother is my wife's mother's cousin. We happen to know Alvin's mother kicked him out last spring. He was stealing her prescription drugs.

"I just got off the phone with Jerry Anderson, his probation officer, who said he didn't show up for his weekly appointment this morning. Jerry made some calls during the day but no sign of the guy. He figures he's on his way to Michigan. The Canadian border is so tight these days, we're pretty sure he won't risk that."

"Okay," said Lew. "Can you take care of putting out an APB on the guy?"

"Already did," said Todd. "Sorry I couldn't do more."

"I'm not," said Lew. "It's been a long day. I'm going fishing."

Chapter Seventeen

Osborne knew better than to try reaching Mallory before six so he busied himself making dinner for the kids and, hopefully, Lew. A large Ziploc bag of chili from the freezer and fresh corn on the cob with a soft stick of butter and slices of delicious cheesy bread from the Loon Lake Market? Yep, that should do it.

By the time he had finished husking the corn, setting the table, and putting the bag of chili in hot water to thaw—the cuckoo clock chimed six.

Surely Mallory would be home by now, he thought as he wiped his hands on a tea towel. On the other hand, even though they had short summer hours at the ad agency where she was a vice president of marketing, he knew she liked to stop by her gym for a workout. Hopefully not today. If he took Beth, Harry, and Lew out on the boat, they might get back too late to call.

It wasn't reasonable but he felt an urgency to get Mallory's input. His abhorrence of Gladys and Cynthia Daniels was pushing him to be more critical than he knew was fair. While he knew Mallory carried a cell phone, this was one conversation he wished to have when she could talk without worry of being overheard.

He dialed her home number. To his relief, after two rings she answered. "Hi, Hon, do you have a minute?" he asked.

"Dad? How are you? What's up? Is this a good call or a bad call?" Mallory rattled off the questions, a hint of caution in her voice. Osborne knew she hoped he wasn't calling with bad news about anyone: himself or Erin, Mark, and any of his grandchildren.

123

Though the sisters got along, they didn't talk often on the phone. Nor did Osborne and Mallory chat more than once a month.

"Research, kiddo. I'm helping Lew out with a sad situation up here. A young woman was found stabbed to death late yesterday afternoon. Jennifer Williams. Did you ever know her?"

"I've known of her but, gosh, Dad, she's ten years younger than I am. Erin might know her better. One of my high school friends used to babysit for her if that would help. Doesn't her mother work at the Loon Lake Market?"

"That's the family. But I'm not calling about Jennifer so much as some of the people who knew her. Jennifer had been running the graphics department at the new clinic where Cynthia Daniels is a trauma physician in the emergency unit. Cynthia is one of the people I'm calling about."

"Right, my best friend. Dad, if there is anyone I avoid with a passion it is Cynthia Daniels. All I know is she somehow managed to get into medical school years ago. Probably slept with the admissions director. So what does she have to do with Jennifer Williams?"

"Well, for one thing they didn't get along—"

"What else is new? Cynthia is all about guys. She is not a 'girl's girl' if you know what I mean."

"I do," said Osborne and grinned into the phone. Once he and Mallory had made their peace after Mary Lee died—finding their way to a friendship that had eluded both while Mallory was growing up—Osborne found her acerbic take on human beings (who deserved it) entertaining and perceptive.

"Remember, Dad, because she was in boarding school I only saw her summers but we sort of hung with the same crowd. When it came to any of us girls, Cynthia had such a nasty edge to her. She would make cutting remarks about your clothes or your figure or your hair—and always in front of the boys, of course."

"Competitive?"

"To put it mildly. But what amazed me was her behavior toward boys. She was s-o-o-o promiscuous. And boys liked her. At eighteen, who doesn't want to get laid, you know?

"The last summer that I saw her, which was after our freshman year in college, she went after this one guy, Greg Cooke, who was a camp counselor at Camp Chippewa. He wanted nothing to do with her. He told me that. In fact, I was dating him that summer—"

"You were dating a boy that Cynthia was interested in?"

"'Interested' is putting it mildly. She was obsessed. She stalked Greg. One night, she drove down a back road into the camp, waited in the woods until he came out and got into a car with a friend. She followed them into town and into the bars, hanging on him even though he asked her to leave him alone. Several times she did that. Creepy.

"That fall, when he was back at the University of Wisconsin, she showed up at his frat house one night. Same routine. I remember he called me totally freaked out."

"How long did Cynthia keep that up? With Greg?"

"About six months. He and I stayed in touch for a while so I know he knew she was lurking around. But he played it cool, didn't respond to her, and the stalking died off eventually. You know, Dad, I haven't talked to Greg in years. Want me to Google him and see if he's around? He was a nice guy. I'd love to know how his life has turned out."

"Sure, if you're comfortable with that. But you've told me enough to give me some perspective on the woman."

"Dad, I feel bad saying so many negative things about Cynthia. I'm sure she's matured and isn't so crazy anymore. After all, I've had my demons, too. You know that."

Yes, he did. And yet, oddly enough, it was through her struggle with alcoholism that he had grown to love her. Or maybe it was the shared struggle that made the difference for both of them. Today, Mallory was a person less perfect than what her mother had wanted. More like him. And he cared for her more deeply than he ever had in her youth.

"Does any of what I've just said help with the investigation, Dad?"

"It does, and the other reason I'm calling is Gladys. The old lady."

"C'mon, Dad, are you trying to ruin my day?"

Osborne chuckled. "No. But here is what's bothering me: Gladys Daniels alleges she saw the man who killed Jennifer Williams. She says she was walking her dog near the condos where Jennifer lived and claims to have witnessed the assault."

"Wow," said Mallory. "Could she see who it was?"

"So she says—and that's just it," said Osborne, heaving a sigh as he said, "I'm having a hard time believing her. This afternoon Lew and I spent over an hour questioning that woman."

"Still the mean old bitch?"

"Oh-h-h, you better believe it. Managed a few jibes at me right off the bat. But back to the fact she alleges she saw the murder take place—or saw the man who killed Jennifer within moments of the assault. Does it surprise you that I'm having a hard time believing her?"

"Yes and no. Yes if she really saw something—or someone. But the woman has always been a vicious gossip and lot of it lies. You remember the crap she spread about me that one summer—when I got kicked off the tennis team thanks to her lies?"

"I'll never forget that," said Osborne.

"What makes you think she might be lying now?" asked Mallory. "I mean, that's a hell of a story to tell if it isn't true."

"After Lew and I heard the details of what Gladys insists she saw, she launched into a series of snide remarks about the murder victim."

"You mean Jennifer Williams?"

"Right. Remarks that were not necessary."

"That is weird. I wonder why?"

"So do I. That's why I've called. You've known both these women since you were a kid. But here's the other issue, Mallory: Can Cynthia be trusted?

"Lew and I are both ready to discount anything Gladys says. We think she's a nut case. Plus, Lew is always hesitant to trust eyewitness accounts."

"That's wise. Recent court cases down here in Illinois prove that. But why are you questioning anything Cynthia says about all this? So what if she didn't get along with that young woman? No reason to murder someone."

"My sense is that Cynthia knows something that can help with the investigation—but so far she has stonewalled us or we've gotten conflicting stories from her and a couple of her colleagues. We understand from one person close to her that Cynthia despised Jennifer. And she has deliberately lied about her whereabouts at the time the murder occurred. Something doesn't fit."

"Dad, when it comes to Cynthia, lying may be genetic. I think Gladys and Cynthia are two of a kind: people who think not getting caught in a lie is the same thing as telling the truth. But I doubt she would commit murder. Why do you need to even deal with her?"

"Good question. Maybe I'm making too much of the fact that Cynthia and Jennifer worked in the same environment and there was bad blood between them. But why would Gladys rant about a young woman she barely knew?

"Gee, Mallory, I'm sorry to bother you with this. The more I talk about it, the more confused my thinking."

"No, it's okay, Dad. You know, what I remember most about Cynthia and her mother was Mrs. Daniels's insistence that Cynthia be perfect. She always had the nicest, most expensive clothes, her folks bought her a convertible when she turned sixteen—and then there was the plastic surgery. Remember that?"

"No, but I do remember Gladys wanting Cynthia's teeth straightened for strictly cosmetic reasons. Her bite was fine and I told her orthodontia might cause more problems than it could fix. When I refused to recommend it, she went to Wausau and had it done anyway. What was the surgery?"

"This was after college, and I only heard about it from friends. Apparently Cynthia had her nose done. Gladys didn't like the result, so she insisted on another nose job. And another. Three nose jobs before she was happy with Cynthia's face.

"Oh, and then there was the abortion."

"What?" All this was news to Osborne.

"During her senior year in college, Cynthia got pregnant. Gladys met with the boy and his parents, didn't like them, said they didn't have enough money and insisted Cynthia end the pregnancy and the relationship."

"Ever hear how Cynthia felt about that?"

"Umm, my impression has always been that she takes orders from the old lady. But that may have changed. She doesn't live with her mom, does she?"

"On the same property. In the guest house."

"Really? Cynthia is in her late thirties, making a ton of money, and *living at home?*"

"I rest my case," said Osborne. "Too many weird elements. Jennifer Williams's death aside, the fact that these two women are in any way connected to the crime just bugs the hell out of me."

"Sorry I can't help you more, Dad. Keep me posted on this, will you?"

After talking with Mallory, Osborne checked the driveway for bikes. No sign of Beth and Harry yet. He checked his watch, looked over Erin's list regarding Beth and her schedule, and decided to follow instructions and check on the status of Beth's cell phone and her texting. After reaching the 800 number and following the prompts in Erin's note, he got the total of text messages sent and received.

He was surprised: Beth's texting over the last two days was less than half what her mother allowed. Well, he wondered, what was Erin worried about?

Then it dawned on him: Beth and Harry were spending too much time together. So close they didn't have to text. Whoa. He better put a stop to that. But how to handle it in a diplomatic "grandfatherly" kind of way? Yikes. He'd ask Lew—she would know.

Osborne set a pan of water on to boil the corn and a sauce pan to heat the chili, and, in spite of the nutritional compromise, he ripped open a bag of tortilla chips to have with a jar of salsa. It might not add years to their lives but at least they would get enough to eat. And he had ice cream bars in the freezer.

The phone rang. "Doc?" asked Lew. "It's just six thirty. Am I too late for dinner?"

Chapter Eighteen

"I figure we have two more hours of light," said Osborne, looking up from where he and Lew were busy organizing the muskie rods and tackle while waiting for the kids. The evening sky was a periwinkle blue streaked with dove gray scribbles: the brushwork of a celestial painter gone berserk.

"I'm bringing one fly rod along," said Lew. "I tied a dry fly this winter that I'm hoping works on big muskies. We'll see. Whose is this?" she said, reaching for a spinning rod that someone had set on the bench at the end of the dock.

"That's young Harry's muskie rod," said Osborne. "After I invited him to go along with us, he biked home and got his own gear." Osborne glanced up toward the house. "What on earth is taking those kids so long? Beth," he hollered, "you and Harry need to get down here. We're ready to go."

"Here we come, Gramps," said Beth, tripping down the stone stairs with Harry close behind.

Even with four fishermen on board, the boat moved easily over the water. Ripples shimmered in the setting sun as Osborne steered up the east shoreline, through the channel, and into the stretch of river connecting the Loon Lake chain.

He slowed as he neared a small bay and cut the motor. The boat rocked quietly in its own wake. With a whoosh, Osborne dropped anchor.

"Doctor Osborne, why are we stopping here?" asked Harry. "My dad said a good muskie fisherman always works the weed beds along the shoreline." The boy looked over both shoulders then turned to Osborne. "This doesn't look right to me."

"Well, Harry," said Lew with an easy grin. "Shore beaters have their virtues, but Doc and I are going for suspended muskies tonight. We're anchored over a forty-foot pool that's fed by a cold spring at the bottom. Just you watch, because if we're lucky enough to hit a window when they're feeding—could be a big girl just waiting for us."

"Forty feet down?" Harry looked dubious.

"Not that deep," said Lew. "She'll be lurking around fifteen, maybe sixteen feet. No wind tonight, so it won't matter which direction you cast."

With a shrug, as if he was willing to try the impossible, Harry pulled a Red RizzoTail out of his tackle box and hooked it on to the end of his fishing line. Standing up behind Beth, he cast toward shore.

Osborne was planning to use his old, reliable bucktail, but first he rigged Beth up with a neon-green crank bait that he knew would stand out in the tannin-stained water. He glanced over to see Lew getting ready to tie on her new muskie fly.

"Check it out, Doc," she said, holding the bright purple dry fly in her hand. "It's my variation of a Rainy Carp Tease, size eight. I added color because of this dark water. It's designed to imitate a dragonfly. Just what a big girl is hungry for—I hope."

Lew grinned over at Osborne. She was so happy fishing. All the strain left her features, her black eyes sparkled, and that smile— there were a great many things he would do for that smile. Fishing came second.

As the boat swayed with their casts, the four murmured in soft voices so as not to spook any monsters below. "So, you two," said Lew, false casting twice before letting the dry fly at the end of her leader soar nearly fifty feet toward the far shore, "Doc said you've been doing basketball camp and biking this week. Either of you got summer jobs?"

"No, darn it," said Harry, "I'm not sixteen yet, so I couldn't apply many places. I wanted to make some money, too."

"Yeah, me, too," said Beth with a cast of her spinning rod that made her grandfather proud. "At least I've been doing some babysitting."

"Where are you biking?" asked Lew. "The highways?"

"No. Off-road, mostly, like the Bearskin, the snowmobile routes, and some of the logging lanes," said Harry.

"Well, keep an eye out," said Lew. "The Forestry Service will pay twenty bucks for any old, rusty machinery or vehicles you might see back in the woods. You find it, they'll pick it up and pay you. Could be some easy money."

"Hey, Beth, you hear that?" asked Harry. "What about that old pickup we saw yesterday—on the bike trail behind the condos? I didn't see anybody around, did you? Maybe somebody just left it there. We should check it out."

"No, Harry, I saw somebody," said Beth. "You'd already gone by but I saw a guy standing a little ways off the trail. Saw him throw some garbage or something. But we should check it out 'cause that was an old truck. We could split the twenty bucks, right?"

"Where was this that you saw the pickup?" asked Lew.

"You know those new condos behind the clinic—we like to ride the trail back behind there because it's so close to school. Easy to get there after practice," said Beth.

"And you were there yesterday?"

"Yeah, right after basketball practice," said Harry. "Me and Beth try to ride every day. To build our endurance." He threw his line out as he talked.

"What time was that—or about what time?"

Harry looked over at Beth, "A little after six wasn't it?"

"I think so. Why, Chief Ferris? Did we do something wrong?"

"No, not at all. But I—"

"Oh my God!" screamed Harry as a huge fish leaped into the air about fifty feet from the boat. His line went slack as the fish charged the boat.

"Keep the pressure on—set the hook! Set the hook!" cried Osborne.

"Ohmygod!" Harry screamed again, rearing back as he threw his fishing rod at the fish. The fish stormed under the boat with Harry's rod close behind. Minutes later the rod surfaced out in the middle of the bay. The Red Rizzo Tail was nowhere in sight. Harry sat stupefied on the boat cushion.

"I can't believe you did that, Harry," said Beth.

Harry gave her a baleful stare. "Oh, yeah? And what would you have done?"

Beth was wise enough not to answer.

"That was a trophy muskie, kid," said Lew. "Minimum forty-five inches. I told you there are some big mothers suspended down there. Next time maybe the fish won't charge the boat so you'll have time to set the hook."

Osborne, who had been rowing in the direction of the floating muskie rod, plucked it out of the water, examined the fishing line where it had been bitten off, and handed the rod to Harry. "You'll want to take that reel apart before the water ruins it." He winked at Harry, "What happens on Loon Lake stays on Loon Lake."

Harry gave a sheepish laugh. For all his fifteen years, he looked five.

Patting the boy's shoulder, Lew said, "First thing in the morning, I want you and Beth to show me where you saw that pickup. Beth, tell me what the man looked like—the one you saw near the bike path. Did you see the direction he threw whatever it was?"

"I saw him throw something but I didn't see his face real good," said Beth. "He was just some guy. He didn't look weird or anything."

"Nothing distinctive?"

"Umm," Beth pondered. "Not really, Chief Ferris. I was too busy watching the trail."

They pulled up to Osborne's dock just as the setting sun was firing the sky with a hazy orange-pink glow. Before his granddaughter clambered out of the boat, Osborne reached for her elbow saying, "Beth, I'd like you to wait here with me. Lew and Harry can carry the tackle up. We need to talk."

Beth gave him a serious look, then sat back down on her boat cushion. She waited quietly until she and Osborne were alone. "You know your mother has been concerned about how much you use your phone for texting, right?"

"Yes."

"But you've only used half of what you're allowed."

"Really?" The girl looked pleased.

"I'm worried that you're spending too much time with this boy." At the puzzled expression on Beth's face, he added, "Harry—your boyfriend."

"Gramps," said Beth in a firm tone. "Harry is my friend. Not my *boyfriend*. I mean we do sports together. Not other stuff. Jeepers, Gramps. *Totally not*." She glanced away embarrassed.

"Well, now, hold on there, young lady," said Osborne, surprised to find himself on Harry's side, "don't discount friendship. The best person to fall in love with is a person you would think of as your best friend. I mean, it's easy to be attracted to someone but to stay attracted you have to have more."

"Okay, Gramps," said Beth, looking antsy. "Is that all? I should go help Harry and Chief Ferris." She tried to stand up but Osborne reached again for her elbow and pressed her back down onto the boat cushion.

He could see she wanted out of this conversation but he knew from experience with his daughters how rare the opportunity is to deliver hard-earned wisdom to a teenager. He decided to plow ahead—*he* wasn't embarrassed.

"Take, for instance, your grandmother and me," he said. "She was a fine woman, and we got married thinking we would get along great. But we never figured out how to have fun *together*. Doing the same things—*together*. So keep that in mind, Beth, sweetie." The child looked stricken. Osborne was sure she was wondering what on earth she had done to deserve this.

"In five or six years, maybe Harry will be your boyfriend. Think about it—you enjoy biking together, playing basketball—"

"No, Gramps, he's on the boys team, I'm on the girls. Really, he is just a friend. And he's goofy."

"I was goofy at sixteen," said Osborne. He winked, "I'm still goofy."

"Grandpa, really, really—he is only a friend."

"Beth, if you are strictly friends, then why aren't you texting like your mom expected?"

"That has nothing to do with Harry—my friend Katie's phone is broken. She dropped it in the school parking lot and her mom won't buy her a new one." Beth looked ready to cry.

"Oh. . . . Is Katie the person you text most of the time?"

"We used to but not right now. Her mom is making her pay for a new phone—or get straight A's next semester—and that's not going to happen." Beth grimaced. "Katie doesn't have much money and, well, she's not that smart."

"So the texting has nothing to do with Harry?"

"Harry doesn't even have a phone . . . yet. He wants one but—"

"It's okay, you run on up now. I'll get the rest of the tackle."

"And I got the boat cushions," said Beth, jumping up and grabbing her cushion. With a helping hand from Osborne, she clambered out of the boat. She stopped and smiled down at him, "Grandpa, I cannot believe Harry threw that rod in the water."

"Well, hon—here's one final tip from an old man who learned the hard way: Let Harry be the one to tell that story."

"I will," said Beth as she turned to dash up the stone stairway to the house.

So Harry is just a friend. Wow, is that a relief! Osborne followed her up the stairs, humming.

They were in bed before ten. "I'll be out of here by six," said Lew, propping herself on an elbow and leaning into him. "Have to see the mayor first thing—can't believe he's demanding a budget report. It's not even the end of the month. Afterward, I'll give you a call. I'd like Beth to show us where she saw that guy throw something. That had to be Alvin and I can't help wondering what he was up to."

"Okay, I'll make sure she waits here. But you're working all day?"

"Planning to take Monday off if all goes well."

"You must be exhausted, Lewellyn."

"If Lewellyn was that tired, she would be in her own bed."

"Oh." Osborne's heart lifted. He knew what she liked and he went there.

Chapter Nineteen

Most people take it easy on Saturdays. Not Chet Tillman. He had left a message that he would be in Lew's face by eight A.M. that morning and, by God, he was five minutes early.

"Coffee, Chet?" Lew asked, standing up to pour herself another cup. She resisted calling him "Mr. Mayor" on principle: she didn't like how he used his office to keep his booze-sodden brother-in-law in the coroner's office—plus she found him to be a pompous ass who only got elected because no one else wanted the job.

"No, Chief," said Chet, leaning back in his chair and spreading his wide, heavy legs. Lew noticed that his summer shirt gaped slightly just above his belt where the belly hung over. She averted her eyes. Chet Tillman's flesh was not appetizing.

"So, budget update?" She found it curious he was staring at his shoes rather than picking up the spreadsheet pages she had printed that morning. Chet had a huge head with graying light brown hair falling over his forehead: the classic fifties male comb-over. His wide, flat face was a pasty shade of pale, and the nosepiece of his rimless glasses was held in place by a wart just above the veined bulb anchoring his nose.

However, beyond having to work around Pecore, Chet didn't give her much grief, so she told herself to tame her critical eye and get on with the budget discussion.

"Hard to estimate the final cost of our investigation of the death of Jennifer Williams, Chet. I've got one of the Wausau boys up here working through the weekend—he's gathering evidence and taking care of DNA analysis for us—"

"I'm not here about the budget, Lewellyn." The unexpected use of her name rather than her title surprised Lew. "I've talked to the law enforcement committee and we want you to take an early retirement. End December."

Lew was speechless.

"The State provides for law enforcement professionals to qualify for full benefits at age fifty." He managed an insincere smile. "I believe you turn fifty shortly. Correct?"

"In October. But I've only worked in the department for seven years and I don't think I—"

Chet shuffled a clutch of papers he had pulled from a flat briefcase. "I took care of that. You've done a super, super job, and the city council is going to vote you a full retirement package—health benefits and all. The details are here." He slapped the papers on the desk in front of her. "Pretty nice, huh?"

"Thank you but no thank you," said Lew, pushing the papers back toward him. "I like this job. I have no intention to retire, but thank you anyway." She stood up from where she was sitting across from him at the conference table and extended her hand to shake his.

"Sit down," he said. Chet hadn't moved and now he leaned forward, "I want you to retire."

"But why? You just said that I've done a 'super, super job.'"

Chet looked down at his shoes again and took a deep breath before saying, "Okay, here's the deal. My son wants to move back to Loon Lake. He's got five years in as a cop over in St. Paul, Minnesota while picking up some graduate credits in criminal forensics and city management.

"He Twitters and he's on Facebook. Lewellyn, he is the new generation of law enforcement, and Loon Lake needs his social media skills."

"Well, I agree with some of what you say," said Lew, "but that is why Dani Spencer has been interning with us until she graduates from the tech college next spring. She Twitters and Facebooks—all those things. Chet, she is a terrific computer geek, and I plan to bring her on board—"

"It's settled, sweetheart," said Chet. "The committee voted last night. I've already told Chet Junior he starts January first."

"Do you want me to leave today?"

Chet gave her a calculating look. "No-o-o, but my son is available as early as November. If we haven't found the person who murdered the Williams woman, might be wise to bring him on. I'll bet with his skills, he could wrap this case in a few days."

Now Chet raised his heavy body from the chair. He shoved the chair in and thrust a beefy hand at Lew. "I knew this would catch you off guard, Chief, but once you think it over you'll be pleased. Heck, I'd like to be in your shoes—full retirement and health benefits at fifty. Wow." He shook her hand and gave a cheery wave as he left the room.

Lew sat at the conference table, thinking. She stood up, walked over to her desk, and hit speed dial on the phone console.

"Dani? Am I waking you? Oh, good. Say, I have an assignment for you to handle when you've got the time. I'd like a full background check on a police officer named Chester Tillman Junior. . . . Right, the mayor's son. I believe he's working somewhere around the cities—his dad didn't say exactly where. . . . Who knows why, the old man's got something up his sleeve.

"Anyway, this is on your own time, and I will pay you for it. This is not official business. . . . Well, I'm being urged to hire him and I want to know more. . . . If you don't have the time please say so. . . . Great.

"And, Dani, this is highly confidential—just between you and me. . . . Good. Thanks, Dani." She speed dialed again: "Doc? Is Beth up yet?"

"She is. We're just finishing breakfast," said Osborne. "I'll drive her into town and we'll meet you out on that logging road where the kids saw the pickup. Be there in ten minutes."

Lew hung up. She stared at the desktop. She felt like she did when someone she loved died: flat.

Doc and Beth were waiting by his car where the logging lane turned off the county road. The turn-off was less than five hundred yards from the drive leading to the condos where Jennifer Williams had been murdered. It was another perfect August morning: the sun bright through the leaves of the aspen crowding the trail, the humidity low, and the sound of birds happy in the brush.

"How far down? Should we drive or park here?" asked Lew through the window of her police cruiser.

"I asked Beth the same question and she thinks we should walk it. She's hoping to recognize the spot where she saw the pickup," said Osborne.

"Good morning, Beth . . . Doc," said Lew, getting out of the car. "Let's go."

They walked in silence, Lew and Doc following Beth. Doc glanced over at Lew. "Hey, you look worried. Something wrong?"

"Not sure," she said. "Tell you later. I want to focus on this right now."

"Okay." Osborne gave her a hard look. In the three years he had known her, she had never responded so curtly. Something was very wrong.

"Right around here, I think," said Beth, pausing to examine the brush and trees along the lane. "Yes, I'm pretty sure. . . ." She walked to the right, turned around to see behind her, and pointing said, "I was riding in this direction when the man had just thrown something that way. His arm was pretty high like this." She mimicked throwing something.

"Had to have some weight to it, I imagine," said Osborne. "Not like he was throwing paper trash."

"Right," said Beth. "Could have been a rock."

"Let's take a look," said Lew as she contemplated a plunge into the wall of young aspen. "Beth, you wait here. Your grandfather and I will check to see if we can find anything. Oh, one more thing—I know I asked you this before but tell me again—what did this person look like? Anything unusual come to mind since we talked last night?"

"Not really," said Beth. "I didn't see his face, and he was dressed normal. Not like he was homeless. Just . . . normal, I guess."

"Good bird hunting in here, I'll bet," said Osborne scanning the woods before picking a spot twenty feet down the road. "I'll start here in order to cover more territory. Don't be surprised if I flush a grouse or two." He hoped his light tone might help to lift the gloom from Lew's face.

The two of them scoured the forest floor, pushing aside clumps of fern and blackberry bushes that managed to grow among the spindly aspens. Twenty feet out from the lane, Osborne spotted something metallic glinting in the sunlight.

"Lewellyn," Osborne raised his voice as he held back the branches of a large shrub. "Come over here, I found something. Not sure what it is. Got nitrile gloves on you?"

"In the cruiser," said Lew, crashing through the brush. She knelt to take a look at the object then got to her feet. "Not a bread knife."

"A scalpel is my guess," said Osborne. "Or a fillet knife."

"Long enough to be the weapon that killed Jennifer," said Lew. "Let me get my evidence kit before we destroy any trace evidence. Doc, you hold the spot, please."

"Right." He waited as she ran down the lane to the cruiser, spoke briefly to Beth who was leaning against his car, and hurried back. "Slow down," said Osborne as she got close.

Gloves on, Lew reached for the knife. "Got it," she said. She grasped the knife by its handle and held it high. "I want to rush this to Bruce. Keep your fingers crossed there's enough tissue or blood on this handle or the blade that he can run a DNA analysis."

Her eyes met Osborne's as she said, "Starting to look like our friend, Alvin Marski, did more than run off with his buddy's truck, doesn't it? But, Doc, even if this knife is the one used on Jennifer Williams, we found no connection between those two. Not yet anyway." Lew shook her head, mystified.

"Could it be a random killing?" asked Osborne. "The kid's been hooked on drugs of some kind. Maybe he was looking for someone to rob and it got out of hand? Or Jennifer was mistaken for someone else?" His questions hung in the air.

"Lewellyn," said Osborne as they headed back toward their cars, "are you going to tell me what's bothering you?"

"I'm being forced out of the department."

"Fired?" Osborne was astounded.

"No. Chet Tillman said the law enforcement committee wants me to take early retirement in December."

"I don't believe this."

She turned sad eyes to his: "It's true."

"Are you—can you—fight it?"

"Not sure yet. Appears they have already offered the position to Tillman's son, Chet Junior."

"Are you kidding?" said Osborne. "I can see bringing him in as a junior officer but to replace you as chief? Doesn't make sense."

"Doc," said Lew, "this is Loon Lake. What else is new?"

Driving Beth back to his house, Osborne puzzled over the knife they had found. He felt he had seen one like that before. A scalpel. Similar to knives used by oral surgeons. Then it dawned on him: taxidermy.

He remembered the wonderful set of knives that Marv Daniels had been given by his colleagues as a retirement gift. Much as he hated to think of talking to Gladys one more time, it might be helpful to ask her to show Lew the set.

Then again, why put himself and Lew through that? Taxidermy is so common in the Northwoods—hundreds of taxidermists must own knives like that. Hell, you can buy them at garage sales.

Chapter Twenty

"Did you hear the one about the mushroom that walked into the bar and ordered a vodka tonic?" asked Ray.

He grinned over at Leigh as they rode back from the shooting range. At the last minute, he had finagled Osborne's Subaru, figuring Leigh might not appreciate riding in his pickup with the hole in the floor and a strong odor of fish.

"No, I have not heard that one," said Leigh with a giggle. She couldn't remember when a man had made her feel so pretty and fun and interesting. "It's not off-color, is it?" She giggled again, not caring if it was or wasn't.

"'We don't serve your kind,' said the bartender." Ray deepened his voice in mock seriousness.

"'*What?*' The mushroom was offended. 'How can you say that? I'm a 'fun-guy.'"

"Oh, you," said Leigh with a punch to Ray's upper arm. "That is *such* a bad joke."

Ray gave her a big smile. It had been a good afternoon. Leigh took instruction well and, after an hour spent learning the correct stance and two-hand hold on his Smith & Wesson .22 target pistol, she had asked him to go with her to Ralph's Trading Post to help her select a gun that fit her hands better.

After settling on a Model 3913 Ladysmith—and a handsome black holster that she liked because it matched her purse—they had returned to the shooting range for another thirty minutes of practice. Leigh surprised him with her aptitude—she was a natural, able to hit the bull's-eye almost every time.

If he hadn't already planned to meet up with Bruce for fish fry that night, he would have lingered. He liked the girl.

"How are the webcams working for you?" asked Ray as he turned into the McNeils' driveway.

"Perfect," said Leigh. "I scrolled through the video on the monitor this morning and it was quite clear—our only visitors last night were a doe and two fawns. I could even make out the spots on the little guys."

"Let's hope those are the only visitors you'll have."

"I'm just relieved that Jim doesn't travel again for a while," she said, opening the car door to get out. "A couple business dinners. Two this weekend in fact. New recruits for the medical staff," she said in response to Ray's raised eyebrows. "You have to talk to those people when they're not on call. But at least he's not out of town.

"Ray, I can't thank you enough for helping me with this. If you'll wait here, I'll get Jim to write a check for your time."

"No, no," said Ray. "You folks are paying me for the webcams and that's enough. Plus," he winked, "this was fun for me, too. Not often do I get to spend an entire afternoon with such a lovely lady."

Leigh felt herself blush with pleasure at the compliment. As she opened the front door to enter her home, she wished it wasn't so easy to learn how to shoot a pistol. Too bad she didn't need another lesson—or a hundred lessons. What a cute guy!

At three o'clock that afternoon Lew sat back at her desk and rubbed her eyes. It had been a long week, but the stack of reports flowing in from the investigation into Jennifer Williams's death was growing—by the moment it seemed.

The desk phone rang: "No, thank you, Doc. I have this paperwork to tackle before I do anything else. I think it best if I'm home alone tonight. Sorry."

"You sure about that, Lewellyn?" asked Osborne. "You might feel better if you bounce Chet Tillman's remarks off me. I might have another perspective or help formulate a rebuttal. Don't forget I have good connections on that city council. Chet may think he runs the show but he doesn't. . . ."

"C'mon, you know I value your input, but right now is not the time. Too much to deal with on the Williams case. Finding that knife has put a whole new spin on things. I'm hoping we can locate our person of interest soon."

"Alvin?"

"Yeah, the sooner the better, y'know. Otherwise Tillman may have enough ammunition to . . . well, to complain." Her voice trailed off and Osborne wished he were in the office to give her a reassuring hug.

"We'll get through this, Lew. And you will keep your job. I promise."

"Thanks, Doc. I appreciate the support. Later, okay?" Lew hung up thinking, Easy for you to say. We'll see. Chet sure has his ducks lined up.

"Chief Ferris?" Dani stuck her head through the door. "You got a minute?"

"Dani, it's Saturday. What are you doing here?"

"You asked me to check on that Chester guy."

"But not on your weekend. You need a life, girl."

"I need a job is what I need," said Dani with a grin. "Plus I love doing this stuff. Got some news if you got a minute."

"Sure. Sit down. I need a break anyway."

"This Chester Tillman guy? He goes by Chet—"

"Just like his old man."

"Right. Well, first of all he's only a corporal—"

"You're kidding. He's not a sergeant or a lieutenant? Just a corporal?"

"Yep. So I went on Facebook to see if he's there and found his page." Dani leaned forward conspiratorially as she said, "Guess what? He friended me!"

"Why would he do that?" asked Lew. "Isn't that for close friends or family?"

"I sent him my profile picture." At the mystified expression on Lew's face, Dani said, "You haven't seen the photo I use on Facebook—"

"Dani, I never have been nor do I plan to be on Facebook."

"It's my best photo ever—I look great." Dani gave a sheepish smile.

"Ah, the light bulb just came on," said Lew. "He's a single guy and you are a pretty girl."

"He's a married guy and I'm a pretty girl," said Dani with an edge. The edge that surfaced often enough to convince Lew that Dani would be a valuable addition to the force when she graduated. Edge is good.

"I'm doing this on my own time, right?" said Dani. "The only reason I say that is 'cause I plan to lurk on this guy's page—find out what else he's up to."

"Whatever you do, do not bridge the privacy laws, understand? I'm not hiring you to break and enter."

"That's too bad," said Dani. "I'm not a bad hacker."

"Dani, use your head. You do not want to get us both in trouble."

"Promise, I won't," said Dani, jumping to her feet. "But cool so far, don't you think?"

"Good work."

After Dani left the room, Lew pondered what she had learned. Would Chet Tillman really bring in a corporal to fill the position of police chief? An individual that low on the chain of command in a metropolitan police department?

Corporals achieve the rank of officer or deputy simply by being on the force for five years—no testing, no interviewing, no proving their competence. The most they have to do is stay out of trouble for five years.

And what kind of guy—married—"friends" pretty girls on the Internet?

Most important was this question: Did she trust Dani to not invade Chester Tillman's privacy? Lew didn't let herself answer that one.

Chapter Twenty-One

It was eleven thirty that night when Kerry Schultz arrived at the clinic to work the midnight to six A.M. shift in the ER.

"Call me Type A," was her mantra when colleagues expressed amazement at her habit of an early arrival for the late night shift, "but I get here early because I want to hear what's on the police scanner and review the record of any patients in the waiting area. I don't like surprises." She didn't add: "Because I have no life."

"Drats," said Kerry, muttering to herself as she checked the roster of MDs working her shift. It did not make her evening to see Cynthia Daniels's name. Just the sight of the woman put her in a foul mood. She made up her mind to soldier through—after all, it was only a six-hour shift.

"Dr. Daniels, any immediate concerns?" asked Kerry, glancing up from the nurses' station when Cynthia arrived five minutes before their shift began.

"No. But I have a sinus headache. I'll go rest my eyes until you need me."

Kerry nodded and looked down the charts. A quiet night so far. The action would start around two A.M. after the bars closed. At the moment all they had was a spider bite and an elderly man who had tripped on his door stoop and dislocated his shoulder. Both were resting. No one was waiting.

Shortly after one, the police scanner crackled with a car roll-over on Highway 17: a teenage couple in possible serious condition. Kerry buzzed Cynthia's pager. No answer. She tried twice then waited five minutes. Ten minutes. Still no answer.

She ran down to the doctors' lounge and knocked on each of the three closed doors. When no one answered, she tried the handles to peek into the rooms in case Cynthia had fallen into a sound sleep. No Dr. Daniels.

When she could wait no longer and the ambulance was less than two miles away, she paged the other surgeon on call. "Sorry to wake you, Tim," said Kerry, "but Dr. Daniels can't be reached and the EMTs think we may have a skull fracture on the way—"

Dr. Tim Donovan lived less than a mile from the clinic. He was there within ten minutes. At two o'clock almost to the second, Cynthia Daniels appeared at the nurses' station where Kerry was on the phone calling the parents of the boy to let them know he was in critical condition.

"Why didn't you page me?" said Cynthia, her voice pitched high and loud as Tim Donovan emerged from the examining room. Cynthia turned around to face the other physician. "This was so unnecessary, Tim. Kerry, you owe Dr. Donovan an apology."

Kerry stared at Cynthia. "I checked the doctors' lounge and every one of the rooms and you were not there."

"Silly woman. Of course I was. I was in number three. Come on, I'll show you." Forcing Kerry to walk in front of her, Cynthia burst through the lounge to the room where she insisted she had been resting. Kerry peered through the doorway. Yes, the bed was rumpled. Yes, Cynthia's overnight bag rested on the chair with her street clothes strewn across the foot of the bed.

"But—"

"But, hell," said Cynthia. "Next time do your job. *Check all the rooms.*"

OK, bitch, you asked for it, thought Kerry as she found her chair at the nurses' station, pretended to be looking for a record on the computer, and waited for her heart to stop pounding. Tim Donovan had given her a sympathetic glance but she could tell he believed Cynthia.

Just you wait, Dr. Daniels. I am making that call.

The call to Loon Lake Chief of Police Lewellyn Ferris might well cost her her job, but the need to make the call had been nagging at her: it was the call that Jennifer Williams deserved.

Chapter Twenty-Two

The musical tones of his cell phone woke Osborne from a deep sleep. He needed a few seconds to realize he wasn't in a dream. Hand fumbling on the lamp table in the dark, he finally found the phone only to see Lew's home number listed as "Missed Call." Worried, he pressed the "Return Call" button. The time: 2:02 A.M. was backlit on the phone.

The last he had heard from Lew was shortly after eleven when she had called to say she was headed home and would catch up with him late Sunday morning. "If I'm lucky, I'll sleep in—I need it," she had said.

"Doc?" the voice on the phone was not sleepy. "I just had a call from the McNeil residence. Leigh saw an intruder on the webcam monitor—"

"Right now? Someone is there now?" Osborne swung his feet onto the floor. Outside his bedroom window, the night was pitch black. He scrambled for his shoes.

"They think so but not sure. I'm getting ready to head over to their place. The webcam picked up a figure lurking near the kitchen windows about a half hour ago. Then, minutes later, the same figure appeared down near the boathouse. Leigh's convinced someone is still on the property, even though Jim said he checked everything out, which he shouldn't have done.

"I told him to sit tight even though he's insisting the images on the monitor are of a bear, not a human."

"Lew, you need a good night's sleep. If you aren't in the car yet, let me get hold of Ray and we'll run over to their place. Ray has experience recognizing what those cameras pick up."

"Good try, Doc. But I'll meet you two there."

Osborne hung up. If he had learned anything in his three years working with Lew, he recognized the tone that means: don't argue.

Ray didn't answer until Osborne's second try. When he did it was obvious he, too, had been sound asleep. Osborne explained the situation at the McNeils. "I'll be right there—pick you up," said Ray.

"Give me two minutes to brush my teeth."

"You got it." Ray was through the kitchen door, the engine running in his pickup, before Osborne had his pants buckled.

Leigh was in a long blue bathrobe, her blonde hair loose around her shoulders and her face tense with worry. Jim had pulled a fleece jacket over gray cotton pajamas. The couple were standing in the front hall foyer, their door locked, until they saw Osborne jump out of Ray's pickup. Lew's cruiser pulled in behind them.

"Okay? Can everyone see?" asked Leigh, once everyone had found a chair to crowd around the kitchen table in front of the video monitor. "Here, Ray, why don't you run it." She handed over the remote control.

"The only reason we happened to see this," said Jim, "is that I got up to use the bathroom and noticed the motion lights on in the driveway. I turned on the monitor thinking I'd see a deer or some other animal out there. That's when Leigh woke up and insisted I call you."

Sure enough, at one twenty that morning a dark shape could be seen leaning over a hydrangea bush under the kitchen window. Anyone looking in would be visible to someone standing at the kitchen sink. Whether the camera was too far away or the moon cast shadows through the nearby trees, all that was visible was the outline of a tall figure in motion.

"Not moving like a bear," said Ray. "My guess is a person. But, I mean, it could be a bear. Just that a bear wouldn't spend time looking in your windows—it wants your bird feeder."

The five of them watched, breath held, as the figure appeared to hover near the window for a long moment. Then it was gone. "Darn the trees," said Ray, "I thought I had the webcams hung closer to the house for a better view."

"We were sound asleep and all the lights were off—not much for anyone to see looking through the kitchen window," said Leigh. "One thing though—I fell sound asleep early this evening. Most nights, I haven't been sleeping that well and I'll come down to the kitchen for a late night glass of milk. If I had seen someone looking in the window, I'd have had a heart attack."

"No, hon, I don't think so," said Jim, patting her hand. "You might scream but no heart attack." Leigh smiled a weak smile.

"I hate to say this, but at least now Jim believes me. Someone really *is* out there. It isn't in my head—"

Jim shot his wife a warning look. "Leigh, I never said that."

"You didn't have to—the look on your face."

"Okay, okay, you two," said Lew. "Ray, can you check out the boathouse?"

Ray fast-forwarded the video to an image that was so shadowed it was difficult to make out any defining details. From Osborne's point of view, they could be looking at a lilac bush. "Ah, that's frustrating," said Ray. "Can't tell much from the video."

"I think it has the same shape as the person by the window," said Leigh.

"Well," said Ray with a kind note in his voice, "when the images get fuzzy like this it's a little too easy to see what you want to see. True for all of us."

"Look, folks," said Lew. "Doc and Ray and I will walk your property and check your boathouse before we leave. I'll also call the sheriff's department and see if they had an officer patrolling the county roads tonight who might swing by and take a look every half hour between now and dawn. Think you can get some rest?"

Leigh and Jim nodded. "I will," said Jim.

"I'll do my best," said Leigh. "Thank you, everyone."

Outside minutes later, Ray pointed to footprints in the mulch around the hydrangea bush under the kitchen window. "Look awful similar to the ones we found in the mud on the dryer. I'll run Bruce out when the sun's up and we'll get a cast."

"Good," said Lew.

They checked the exterior of the boathouse, turned on the interior light, and gave the rowboat and the speedboat a good look. Nothing.

"I'd call this a yacht not a speedboat," said Ray leaning into the cabin of the speedboat. "You can sleep four in here. Wonder what this sucker cost? Fifty thousand buckaroos if it cost a dime. Wonder if he takes it out much?"

"Enough boat talk," said Lew. "Not much else we can do right now."

"I agree," said Osborne. "If there was someone on the property, they are long gone now. Bedtime, Lewellyn."

"Gosh, yes, Doc. We'll talk in the morning."

"Not to keep any one a minute longer," said Ray, "but I am hosting Bruce to dinner tomorrow. That halibut I got from my clients who were up in Alaska. Any takers among the jabones standing here?"

"You betcha," said Lew and Osborne in concert.

Chapter Twenty-Three

A wash of apricot softened the evening sky. Straight out from Ray's dock the setting sun left a trail of diamonds glittering as if lighting the way for a fairy princess. To judge from the expression on Ray's face as he passed a plate of sautéed walleye cheeks to his female guests: that fairy princess might be Leigh.

Nor did she appear to mind the attention.

"Got one more person coming," Ray had announced when Lew and Doc strolled down his sandy drive from Doc's house.

"Bruce?" said Osborne. "You said you were inviting him."

"Well, actually, Leigh called with a question on the webcam and I invited her, too."

"Oh, and Jim?" Lew had grimaced and caught Osborne's eye. An evening with friends was beginning to sound like work.

"No, Leigh said he has a business dinner tonight. After that he's taking the group for a cruise on that boat of his. I could tell she was feeling left out so—"

Lew raised a hand, "Rescuing a damsel in distress." She turned to Doc, "Haven't we heard this one before?"

And so Ray's halibut picnic had turned into a gathering of five: Bruce, Lew, Doc, Ray, and Leigh. It was a happy, relaxed group as everyone appeared to have decided to set the real world aside and relish the evening.

Standing with a plate of walleye cheeks in one hand and a bottle of Spotted Cow beer in the other, Leigh Richards was peppering Bruce with questions on his work at the crime lab. Nearby, listening as the two spoke, Ray hovered over his charcoal grill with its foil-wrapped slabs of halibut.

Every few minutes, Ray would interrupt with a question of his own. Seated by Ray's fire pit in a pair of green plastic Adirondack chairs, Lew and Doc sat listening to the threesome's easy banter.

Osborne was relieved to see Lew relax at last. She had said little about her conversation with Chet Tillman. If the evening continued to go this well, maybe he could get her to open up. He knew from his own experience sometimes just talking things over made them much less disturbing.

"You've been watching too much television," said Bruce with a snort after one of Leigh's more egregious assumptions of how DNA technology worked. "That's not real life. That's Hollywood's idea of DNA analysis. Day-to-day lab work is much more mundane. Trust me, DNA analysis does not happen in thirty minutes."

"Really?" asked Leigh. It was Osborne's turn to catch Lew's eye: they could see Leigh was tickled by the attention she was getting. She turned to them, "Chief Ferris, I didn't see the news today—do we know who killed that young woman from the clinic?"

"Still working on it," said Lew in a matter-of-fact tone designed to put an end to that discussion.

"Oh, sorry I brought it up," said Leigh, "you're off duty and I should know better."

"That reminds me," said Bruce beckoning to Lew with a wave. "Chief, something I should share with you. I'm hoping to hear from a buddy of mine working at the lab tonight." He walked over, leaving Leigh to focus on Ray. "Do you mind? Just take a minute."

"C'mon, what did I just say about work?" said Lew, getting to her feet with a chuckle and following him a short distance up the drive.

Bruce spoke quietly as he said, "I found an envelope on the floor of the stolen pickup and I hope you don't mind that I sent it off for a detailed DNA analysis. It didn't fit with everything else I found in the truck.

"I had fingerprints all over the vehicle that belong to the owner and plenty on the gear shift and steering wheel matching Alvin Marski. But the envelope was light blue and made from a heavier stock like you would find with expensive stationery. It was clean, too, so it hadn't been there long."

Lew studied Bruce's face. "Are you thinking that's the kind of envelope that a woman might use?"

"It reminded me of my mom's stationery," said Bruce. "And it appeared to have been sealed. If we're lucky we may get DNA off the saliva."

"I'm glad you sent it off. Certainly worth checking into," said Lew. "Any news from the pathologist handling the autopsy on Jennifer Williams?"

"Nothing yet. I'm expecting a report first thing Monday. The knife has been sent down to the lab, and Ray and I took photos and a casting of the footprints at the McNeil house this morning."

"When are you heading back to Wausau?"

"Tomorrow, but I'll be back up Tuesday. Taking the day off to try out that fishing kayak of Ray's."

"Oh no, he's roped you into that, too?" Lew laughed. At that moment her cell phone rang. It was an unfamiliar number. "Excuse me, Bruce," she said, "tell the group I'll be right back as soon as I get rid of this call."

"Don't keep the halibut waiting," said Bruce, shaking a warning finger.

"Chief Ferris here," said Lew as he walked off.

"Chief Ferris, this is Kerry Schultz—from the clinic. Sorry to call you on a Sunday—"

"That's okay, Kerry. What's up?"

Lew listened to the woman's story and when she had finished, said, "This is very helpful. I'm glad you called. Are you confident all this is true?"

Kerry's answer prompted a nod from Lew. "Good. I appreciate your telling me this, Kerry. If it turns out to have a bearing on the case, are you prepared to testify?" Again she listened. "Thank you, Kerry. After I write up everything you've told me, I'd like to run it by you for accuracy. I'll be in touch first thing in the morning."

Lew walked down to the picnic table where Ray was in the midst of serving the halibut, French fries, and a plate of sliced homegrown tomatoes. Leigh heaped her plate high and giggled at some remark from Ray. It was a happy look that would be short-lived.

Lew glanced over to see Osborne watching her with concerned eyes. She gave a slight nod and voiced the word "Later."

"Kerry Schultz, the nurse from the clinic who was Jennifer's close friend, called while I was talking to Bruce," said Lew in a low voice as she and Osborne stood on Ray's dock watching the sun disappear behind the pines on the far shore.

From the house trailer up behind them came the sounds of Bruce's hearty laughter mingled with Leigh's bubbly chatter as the two helped Ray clean up the dinner dishes.

Osborne waited, aware that Lew's face said it all: Kerry had delivered disturbing news.

"Jim McNeil has been having an affair with Cynthia Daniels," said Lew. "For at least six months that Kerry is aware of. He tried breaking it off a month ago."

"Hmm," said Osborne. He recalled Cynthia's anger in McNeil's office. "Why am I not surprised?"

"He'd been sleeping with Jennifer Williams these last few weeks. Kerry said she felt awful telling me something her friend had told her in strictest confidence, but she can't help thinking Cynthia's behavior these last few weeks might be tied to Jennifer's death. Called Cynthia a pathological liar."

"A family tradition," said Osborne. "What do you plan to do?"

"Nothing tonight," said Lew. "I'll deal with it in the morning." She turned toward the sounds of hilarity coming out of Ray's trailer. "I wonder how much Leigh knows about her husband."

"She can't be too stupid," said Osborne.

"O-o-o-h, I don't know about that, Doc. We can all be as stupid as we need to. . . ."

And don't I know that, thought Osborne.

Half an hour later as they were sitting around the bonfire toasting marshmallows, Leigh's cell phone rang. She spoke into it briefly then hung up. "Jim's not taking the boat out after all. They're all having one more nightcap at the club."

"Looks like I'm going home to an empty house," she said, sounding like a little girl.

"I'll follow you," said Bruce, "make sure you get in okay."

"No, I'll follow her," said Ray. "Gives me a chance to check those webcams, make sure they're working."

Chapter Twenty-Four

As Leigh pulled her car into the garage, Ray noticed Jim's vehicle was not there yet. Good, hardly a burden to keep her company for another thirty minutes or so. Ray pulled past the garage to park in the far corner so his pickup would not be in the way.

Getting out of the truck and looking past the house down toward the lake, he saw a light on in the boathouse.

"Leigh," said Ray, stopping her as she started to open the front door. "Your husband may be back—I see lights on in the boathouse."

"But his car isn't here," said Leigh. She finished opening the door, set her purse on a table in the foyer, and walked back out to stand next to Ray. Her shoulder brushed his and he didn't move away.

"Hey, you're right," she said, starting down the lawn with Ray behind her. "But I tried him on his cell phone a few minutes ago and he didn't answer. Maybe he turned it off by accident?"

As they got closer, Ray heard a grinding noise as if a motor was turning over and over and not catching. It didn't sound right. "Someone's having trouble with the inboard?" he asked as Leigh opened the door.

"Oh God," she backed away both hands to her face. "Oh God."

Ray pushed past her through the open door. To the far right against the wall, the cabin cruiser was tilting at an odd angle while the gears for the boatlift struggled to mesh. Caught in the gears was something black and red: something no longer human.

Ray dashed across the deck, past the dangling boat to the switch on the wall behind the boat. He flipped it down and all was quiet.

With a soft plop, something fell into the water. The water turned crimson.

Osborne and Lew arrived within minutes, an ambulance with three EMTs close behind. As the EMTs raised the bloody mass entangled in shreds of dark cotton, they watched, hoping to identify the victim. No luck. The gears had been churning long enough to eradicate any human features. It was impossible at this point to tell if it was a man or woman.

"Only thing I've ever seen like this," said one of the EMTs, "is that guy who fell in a wood chipper a few years back." One by one the EMTs took turns stepping outside for a breath of fresh air or to vomit.

After calling Todd and Roger for help searching the area for any sign of who the victim might be—and calling in support from the sheriff's office—it was a sheriff's deputy who located the car.

It had been parked on an access road used by the power and light company to service a transmitter for the neighborhood. The road ran along the far side of the McNeil property and was hidden behind a grove of spruce trees. A woman's purse and a set of keys lay on the front seat of the unlocked car. In the purse was a Wisconsin driver's license issued to a thirty-seven-year-old female: Cynthia Daniels, M.D.

Meanwhile, calls to Jim McNeil's cell phone continued to go unanswered. The bartender at the country club said that he had left an hour earlier with several other men. As it was, he didn't arrive home until after the EMTs had left with the corpse.

"What the hell?" he asked, running down to the boathouse, which was now well lit both inside and out. Police and sheriff's vehicles clogged his driveway, including a van from the television station.

"Please stand back, Jim," said Lew as he came running at her. "We have an accident victim, maybe a crime scene. Please, you can't go there—let everyone do their jobs—"

"Leigh? Is Leigh all right?"

"She's up in the house. She's been trying to reach you."

"Sorry. I just realized my phone was turned off—been that way since a meeting late this afternoon. I am so sorry about that."

Lew waved off the apology. "You and I need to talk," she said, "in private. Let's take some time up there on the patio."

"Right now? Can it wait?"

"No."

At that moment Lew's cell phone rang. The switchboard operator for the sheriff's department had official confirmation from the DOT that the car parked on the access road was licensed to Cynthia Daniels.

"Excuse me, Chief Ferris," said a woman's voice from behind Lew as she ended the phone call. "I want to hear what Jim has to say, too."

Lew whirled around. She hadn't heard anyone coming. "Leigh, no. I have questions for your husband—not you. We'll talk later."

"Please," said Leigh. "This is a horrible accident that has happened on our property—property that belongs to me, too. I want to hear everything and I want to hear it now."

Lew gave her a long, hard look. "My questions are not all about this accident."

As if a heavy weight had been lifted, the woman's shoulders straightened. "I know that," said Leigh in a soft tone. "I've known for a long time that things are not right here. Please. . . ."

"Jim?" Lew looked over at McNeil. "Do I have your permission to include your wife in this discussion?"

Head down and staring at his feet, Jim nodded. He knew what was coming. "Okay, you two, if you are not too cold in this night air, let's talk up on the patio."

Chapter Twenty-Five

The halogen lights from the side of the house turned the patio with its round table and four chairs into a surreal version of an interrogation booth. The EMTs had left and only Ray and Bruce remained down at the boathouse where they cordoned it off until morning.

"I'll be here first thing in the morning, Chief," said Bruce. "Left a message for the lab that we had a new development and not to expect me in the office."

"You both look exhausted," said Lew addressing both Ray and Bruce. "Go home, get some sleep, and we'll sort all this out in the morning."

At Lew's request, Osborne had settled into the fourth chair on the patio. Feeling fatigued—it was after three A.M.—he felt the best he could do right now was listen hard and take notes.

"Jim," said Lew, "tell me about your relationship with Dr. Daniels. Her car was found parked on the access road on the other side of those trees," Lew pointed in the direction of the trees. "Her purse was there, other personal items. Her mother was called and confirmed that she was not at home—nor was she at the clinic.

"We believe the remains found in the boathouse are those of Cynthia Daniels."

Twisting his head from side to side as if to deny what Lew had just said, McNeil erupted: "That woman—that woman keeps barging into my life! A month ago I thought I made it clear we were over. She seemed to understand . . . then."

Sitting across from her husband in a chair pushed back from the table, Leigh asked in a voice so firm it surprised Osborne: "Jim, how long had this one been going on?"

171

"Hold on," said Lew. "Leigh, please, no more questions. I'm willing to let you sit in because we haven't determined the nature of Dr. Daniels's . . . accident—but I have to be the one to ask the questions." Leigh nodded.

"Back to your wife's comment," said Lew. "Have there been others, Jim? More women than Cynthia?"

"Yes." McNeil pursed his lips. "One before Cynthia and . . ."

Leigh looked off into the dark, and Osborne got the distinct impression her husband's philandering came as no surprise.

"I became involved with Cynthia about nine months ago," said Jim. "We got together during a national health conference in San Diego. Didn't take long before I knew I'd made a mistake—"

"Why is that?" asked Lew.

"She wanted too much. She invaded my life. Always e-mailing, following me around. She would show up uninvited at clinic business meetings, staff luncheons. I'd go into the cafeteria and she'd be across the room. The woman was smothering."

Jim leaned across the patio table, hands clenched. "I can see today she was unbalanced. But I've known jealous women to do stuff like that. Just took awhile to realize how extreme she was. God, what was I thinking?" He threw his hands high and sat back in the chair.

"You were concerned she would do what?" asked Lew. "Call your wife?"

"Yes. I don't want a divorce. Believe it or not," he raised desperate eyes to meet Leigh's: "I love you. I'm sorry I'm such a . . . such a fool." He broke into sobs.

Leigh sat still. "Little late," she muttered. "Sorry," she said with a glance at Lew.

"Back to earlier this evening," said Lew, pen poised over her notepad, "how did Dr. Daniels know where you would be tonight?"

McNeil struggled to pull himself together. He wiped at his nose and face with a handkerchief. "I, um, one of the techs at the clinic told me she's been accessing my secretary's computer—and my schedule. The woman is not stupid—she is very smart. That's what makes her a good physician."

Leigh snorted.

"So your schedule for today—"

"Included nine holes of golf, then dinner at the club and a twilight cruise back here on my boat. I imagine she planned to surprise me. She did it a couple times early this summer."

"With a happier ending I assume," said Lew. Jim dropped his head.

"The other women. Who were they?"

Osborne noticed a slight hesitation before Jim said, "Woman. Two years ago, I had a brief relationship with one of our bookkeepers, Corrine Jensen. She's since moved to Appleton."

"That's everyone?" asked Lew.

"Yes."

"Jim, I have to ask you this question: did you kill Cynthia Daniels?"

"No, of course not," said Jim with a weak laugh. "If anyone has any doubts, I can account for every minute of my time from four o'clock this afternoon until I got here. . . ."

"Do you think Cynthia Daniels was capable of murder?"

"You must be kidding—she's in the business of healing people. Now, do I think she was capable of stalking me? Yes. The awful thing is she had me convinced that Leigh was the crazy one."

"May I say something?" asked Leigh. Lew nodded for her to go ahead. "Jim's not the only person who thought I was crazy. For months I've thought I was losing my mind. I am not exaggerating when I tell you that suicide has crossed my mind.

"I've had this horrible feeling in the pit of my stomach. I've been having panic attacks and—who knows? If things had gotten much worse . . . That Daniels bitch almost pulled it off."

"Thank you, Leigh," said Lew. "One last question, Jim—and I know we're all tired, so I'll be brief. Has there been another woman *in the past month* with whom you have been intimate besides Cynthia?"

McNeil shook his head "no."

Lew sighed. "That's not what I have heard from a credible source. One of your colleagues. . . ."

"All right, okay—Jennifer Williams."

Leigh gasped and pushed her chair back farther.

"Had you ended that relationship?"

"No." McNeil's voice was a whisper.

"Did Dr. Daniels know about Jennifer?"

"I don't know. Maybe. I know she had nothing good to say about her."

The patio was very still. Only the sound of a distant cricket.

"Do you know who killed Jennifer Williams?" asked Lew.

"Oh my God no. I wish I did."

"Did you kill Jennifer Williams?"

Leigh sucked in her breath.

"No."

"When was the last time you saw her?"

"Half an hour before she left for home the other day. The night she was killed."

That was it for Leigh. Reaching for a glass of water on the table, she stood and hurled it at her husband. He ducked, but it bounced off his head and shattered on the patio cobblestones. Leigh turned and walked off without a word.

"We're finished here for the time being," said Lew, getting to her feet.

Before Lew and Osborne had reached Lew's cruiser, the front door opened. Leigh was framed in the light of the foyer. "Here," she said in a loud voice to the person behind her, "I'm throwing your travel kit in the front yard. You can get your clothes in the morning."

"Leigh, please," they could hear Jim's voice, "you'll be alone. You need me—"

"I need a goddamn lawyer is what I need. *Get out!*"

"Let's scoot, Lew—before we have another crime scene," said Osborne, tugging on Lew's sleeve.

It was nearly four in the morning when Osborne reached to turn out the lamp on the night table. He turned to Lew. "Why on earth didn't Jim McNeil tell us up front about Jennifer? What was he thinking?"

"The man's been lucky too long," said Lew. "I'm sure he's lied to his wife their entire marriage. From what we've learned about Jennifer, with the exception of her close friendship with Kerry Schultz she was pretty much of a loner. I imagine he thought she kept their relationship a secret. He was hoping to get away with it."

"How did he keep it from his wife?"

"Oh, Doc, we are all guilty of seeing only what we want to see. Those two lead parallel lives. I imagine the intimacy of friendship has been missing from that marriage for a long time."

Osborne thought that over. She was right of course. He had been there himself: there are times when confronting reality can be too much to bear.

One goodnight kiss later, Dr. Paul Osborne and Loon Lake Police Chief Lewellyn Ferris were sound asleep.

Down near Osborne's dock, a mother duck guided her brood toward the overhanging boughs of a white pine and tucked her head under one wing. The little ones did the same. Over at the McNeils waves lapped lightly under the boathouse. A pink stain colored the sand along the shoreline.

In the Daniels mansion, Gladys lay in bed: eyes wide open.

Chapter Twenty-Six

Late Monday afternoon Bruce poked his head through the doorway to Lew's office. "Got some reports in, Chief. Do you have a minute?"

"I do," said Lew, pushing aside the letter she had been studying. It was from Chet Tillman asking her to sign off on the city's agreement for her retirement: benefit details, termination date.

The mayor had set a deadline for her to sign and return the agreement by the end of the month, not quite two weeks away. Lew resisted the urge to sign off and be done with it. That was the easy way out. That was something a girl would do.

Setting her jaw, Lew decided to complete the investigation into Jennifer Williams's death—then concentrate on how to fight city hall. She'd done it before and won.

"Okay, what have we got?" said Lew with a welcoming wave. Bruce loped through the door, took a seat in front of Lew's desk, and, crossing his right leg over his left knee, he opened the first of three files.

"The autopsy report on Jennifer Williams doesn't offer much. She died of a stab wound that pierced her heart. No defense wounds, no trace evidence—just clean-cut edges with no bruising. We're assuming the victim was caught by surprise."

"What about the knife wound? Any defining characteristics?" asked Lew.

"No, sorry. The exact details of the wound are in here," said Bruce, handing over a manila file. "As I expected, it's not possible to confirm that the knife you found was used to inflict the wound."

"Okay," said Lew, "what's next?"

"The accident in the boathouse. I'm sure the insurance company will send their own investigator, but I took a good look and I can tell you what I think happened."

"Thanks, Bruce. I'll arrange for the department to pay for your time. We'll call it 'death under suspicious circumstances.'"

"Only if it's easy, Chief. I know you're under a lot of pressure."

"You heard, huh?"

"Doc mentioned something to Ray."

"Well, we'll see how it goes. Tell me what you found."

"My best guess—and it's a good one—is the woman was wearing a beach-type dress, kind of long and flowing. No underwear, no swimsuit. The dress appeared to have snagged on the lift gears as she was climbing into the boat and in trying to yank it loose, she accidentally tripped the 'On' switch. Happened in an instant: the force pulling her into the gears was relentless. That boatlift is designed to hold heavy boats thirty feet long. It does not ask questions."

"Whew," said Lew. "Hell of a way to go."

"One thing you need to know—I had a call this morning from the crime lab. The victim's mother is insisting on an autopsy and a criminal investigation. She is insisting her daughter was pushed."

"What do you think?"

"I see no sign of foul play. That would assume premeditation, and I don't see how that could fit with the sequence of events. But . . ." said Bruce with one of his signature blinks, "her allegation may make it easy for you to cover my time."

He opened the third file with a smile of satisfaction, "The good news is—and I leaned on a buddy of mine to rush the DNA analysis through for no cost so long as I promise to take him out on the Rainbow Flowage next time I'm up north—the blood on the broken glass found in the McNeils' basement laundry room belonged to Cynthia Daniels.

"And that," he said with a waggle of his right index finger, "is not all. The footprint in the mud on the clothes dryer is a match to the pattern on the bottom of one of Dr. Daniels's running shoes. Same for the footprints outside the kitchen window night before last: exact matches. I even have some of the dirt from the bottom of the shoes being analyzed to see if it matches the mix of soil and mulch on the McNeil property."

"So we can tie Cynthia Daniels to the stalking of McNeil's wife but not to the death of Jennifer Williams. No link there—correct?"

"Not that I have found. I've initiated a search of Dr. Daniels's home and office but nothing yet. I will say that mother of hers is a hawk. When I went into the cottage where Cynthia Daniels has been living, back behind the family's big house—she tried to follow me in. I made her stay behind the police tape but she never took an eye off me. That old woman is fierce."

A knock on the door caused Bruce and Lew to look up at Dani, who started into the room, an open laptop braced on one arm. "Chief Ferris, I found something you might find interesting—"

"Pertinent to the Jennifer Williams case?" asked Lew.

"No, but—"

"Later, Dani, I'm busy with crime lab reports right now. I'll get back to you."

"But—"

"Dani, you heard me. I'll get back to you when I have the time."

Bruce got to his feet. "That's everything I got so far. You locate that Marski guy yet?"

"No," said Lew. "His probation officer called this morning to say he's still missing. If he doesn't show soon, he'll be looking at an extended sentence. Meantime, I've got Dani e-mailing his photo to every convenience store in a four-state region: the guy is bound to run out of cigarettes.

"The only other major development I've had is that Doc checked with the clinic staff late this morning and it appears that Cynthia

179

Daniels's absences from the clinic—whether she was on call or not—coincide with the hours during which an intruder was spotted in or near the McNeil home. At least I've got that one solved," said Lew with a weak smile.

"Hey, Chief, in my book—you're doing great. Day off tomorrow?"

"Day off or die," said Lew with a wide grin.

"Isn't that the Wisconsin state slogan?" Bruce chuckled at his own joke.

After Bruce left, Lew braced her elbows on the desk and stared down at the reports that he had delivered. She sat there thinking, not reading. Finally she picked up the phone and dialed Dani's extension. "Would you come in here a moment?" asked Lew.

The girl appeared so fast Lew was startled. "Okay, Chief, you ready for me to show you this?" asked Dani, her eyes eager as she held out her open laptop.

"Not that, not yet, I don't have time for that right now—but I have something I'd like you to get on right away, please. Here's the phone number for Dr. Daniels's secretary, Brenda," said Lew, handing her a slip of paper and ignoring the disappointment in Dani's eyes. "I'd like you to call her ASAP and ask her to forward to you any e-mails that Dr. Cynthia Daniels may have sent to Jennifer Williams."

"Okay," said Dani. "Is this legal?"

Lew sighed. "If she gives you any trouble, I'll have to get a warrant. But I suspect she'll be happy to share anything that shows Dr. Daniels in a bad light. One other reason for her to cooperate is that I doubt she wants her superiors in the clinic to know that she saved those e-mails."

"Right," said Dani. "I see what you mean. Chief Ferris, I have another suggestion. Should I ask if she has e-mails that Dr. Daniels may have sent to other parties *about* Jennifer Williams?"

"Good idea. What I'm looking for is any evidence linking Cynthia Daniels directly to the victim. Right now all we know is that people working around those two women were aware that Dr. Daniels disliked Jennifer. But not liking someone is very different from taking their life."

Now the hard part, thought Lew once Dani had left her office. She picked up the keys to her squad car and told Marlaine where the switchboard could find her. "I'll be gone for an hour at least," she said.

Bonnie Williams was waiting at her front door. "Chief Ferris, please come in. Thank you for calling ahead," she said. "Have you found the person who—"

"No," said Lew, "but we're close. I, um, you and I need to talk. May I sit down?"

"Of course." Bonnie gestured toward a sofa that stood along one wall of the small living room. She took the rocking chair, which was at one end. Judging from the worn cushion, Lew could tell it was her favorite chair. And it faced a large screen TV that anchored the room.

Catching Lew's glance at the television, Bonnie said, "Pretty big for the room, I know. Jennifer bought it for my birthday. She loved to come over and watch *American Idol* with me."

"Nice," said Lew as she sat forward on the sofa. She dropped her head for a long moment, debating where to start. She looked up and plunged in.

"First, you'll be relieved to hear that the crime lab has released Jennifer's body and it should arrive at the funeral home late this afternoon."

"Okay," said Bonnie. "I appreciate knowing that. My sister has been helping me with the arrangements."

Lew tried not to let the mention of the sister, Chet Tillman's wife, distract her from the difficult news she had to deliver. "Bonnie, I am afraid that what I have to tell you may be very upsetting—"

"Chief Ferris, Kerry Schultz came by this morning and told me. She felt that as Jennifer's best friend, she should be the one to tell me the . . . the details." When Bonnie stumbled over her words, Lew knew she was referring to the affair between Jennifer and McNeil, which would have been news to her.

"So, ah," Bonnie sighed heavily as she spoke, "when Kerry heard that Cynthia Daniels was killed in that accident at the McNeil house, she figured that my daughter's relationship with Mr. McNeil would have to become public." Bonnie paused, then said, "Kerry is convinced that Dr. Daniels was jealous and killed Jennifer."

"Hold on," said Lew. "Please don't jump to that conclusion. And I apologize—I didn't realize that the EMTs removing Dr. Daniels's body would have shared the news of the tragedy with Kerry and the other staff in the clinic's ER. I understand Kerry's reason for telling you, but it is confidential information. At this time, we have no evidence linking Dr. Daniels to your daughter's death," said Lew. "Yes, she was jealous. But is she guilty of murder? Bonnie, I am so sorry but we do not know that for a fact.

"I can imagine how you must feel but—"

"No, you cannot imagine how I feel," said Bonnie, her face turning red as she gripped both arms of the rocking chair. "You can have no idea how I feel. First I lose my daughter, now I find she was having an affair with her boss? My Jennifer was a good girl. A good . . ." Bonnie's hand flew to her mouth but the gesture was hopeless.

The woman broke into sobs. Getting up, Lew walked over to the rocking chair where Bonnie sat hunched over, her shoulders shaking. Lew knelt to put her arms around Bonnie. She held her until the shaking eased.

"Bonnie," said Lew, murmuring in her ear. "None of us gets through life without making mistakes. Who is to say what went on between your daughter and Jim McNeil? He may have promised to leave his wife for her. There may have been something honest and deep and wonderful between them. We don't know Jennifer's side of the situation, and that makes it unfair for any of us to pass judgment."

"My Jen was so young," said Bonnie through tears. "He took advantage of her. Excuse me while I find a Kleenex."

She got up, left the room for a minute, and returned with a box of tissues. Lew sat quiet on the sofa until Bonnie had composed herself.

"You're right, of course," said Bonnie. "I'm just thinking . . . well, I'm deeply embarrassed for myself and for Jennifer. Everyone will know. That's what I hate. They'll think so much less of my little girl." She broke down again. Again Lew waited.

"All right, Bonnie," said Lew. "I am going to share some information in confidence. Can I trust you to keep these details to yourself until there is an official release of the circumstances surrounding the accidental death of Cynthia Daniels?"

After pressing several Kleenex to her eyes, Bonnie nodded. Lew offered a more detailed description of Cynthia's stalking of the McNeil home. When she had finished, Bonnie sat straighter in her chair: surely the news of Cynthia Daniels's obsessive actions would overshadow anything her daughter had done.

"So you aren't alone, Bonnie," said Lew. "Think how Gladys Daniels must feel."

Bonnie wiped away a tear. "At least my Jennifer is not guilty of a crime. An affair with a married man, yes, but she didn't hurt anyone. Physically, I mean."

"Why do you say that?" asked Lew, choosing not to mention that Jim McNeil's wife might not feel too kindly toward Jennifer.

"The stalking. I can't believe a physician behaving like that— how awful."

"Gladys will be receiving some harsh news," said Lew. "It won't be easy for her. Nor is it for you. But that's why, given what we know of Cynthia's actions over the past few months, I need to ask if you are aware of any meetings or phone calls or communications of any sort that Jennifer may have had with Cynthia Daniels—inside or outside the clinic?"

"Not that I can think of," said Bonnie. "Is it important?"

"Could be," said Lew. "If you come across anything, please call me right away. Here's my card with my cell phone number."

As she left Bonnie's home and walked toward her police cruiser the strange parallels between the two widows struck her: both had lost their husbands, now both lost daughters who—just days ago—were young women of such promise. And for both Bonnie and Gladys the circumstances surrounding the loss of their children were so grim.

Back at her desk, Lew was pleased to find a memo from Dani with copies of two e-mails attached. She had been able to reach Brenda at her new position, and Brenda was more than happy to forward the only two e-mails that Dr. Cynthia Daniels had sent to Jennifer Williams.

The first was a response to Jennifer trying to set up a photo shoot in the emergency room. All it contained were times that Dr. Daniels would be available. That e-mail was sent in March.

The second e-mail, sent in July, was more to the point: "Bitch, you don't know what you're getting into. Leave Jim McNeil alone. He's mine. Keep it up and you'll find yourself without a job." It was unsigned.

Chapter Twenty-Seven

After an early morning round of verbal wrangling, Osborne was able to persuade Lew to take the day off: "We promised Ray we would try the fishing kayaks. He's counting on us—"

"He's got Bruce, Doc. He doesn't need me."

"I need you. Please, Lewellyn, do not abandon me to the shenanigans of those two. You deserve a break—you have been going full tilt since last Tuesday. Even the good Lord gets a day off."

"Okay, but on one condition—I log two hours in my office this morning. If I can make a tiny dent in the paperwork from the Wausau Crime Lab, I'll be able to relax."

"Deal. I'll pick you up at ten A.M. sharp."

Lew was waiting in the parking lot with her rod case, gear bag, a happy look on her face—and no uniform. She had changed into her fly fishing shirt, sleeves rolled up, and khaki shorts. "We're kayaking the river, right?" she asked as she climbed into Osborne's Subaru.

"Yep. Ray gave me directions to where he wants us to put in. I haven't been there before. You?"

"Nope. Doc, I've only kayaked once in my life. Don't let me do anything stupid like tip over."

"That makes two of us. Can't be that difficult—my grandchildren kayak all the time. They prefer kayaks over canoes."

Twenty minutes later and north of town, Osborne drove down a rock-strewn country road, made two left turns, and pulled into a clearing behind Ray's pickup. Bruce and Ray had already unloaded the four kayaks, which were red, yellow, blue, and green.

"These are twelve-foot recreational kayaks," said Ray, "nice and stable. See the bungees on the sides? They're rigged to hold your rods and plenty of space in the interior for tackle."

"Will I need this?" asked Lew, holding up a long, black MIL-TEC bag with a roll top designed to keep gear and belongings from getting soaked in the event of a swamping.

"Chief, this isn't Niagara Falls. You can throw everything you need onto the floor of your kayak. Do not worry about tipping over. I put our shore lunch in a plastic bag but that's all."

Bruce ran up from the landing where he had left two of the kayaks ready to go: half in the water, half on shore. He watched as Lew assembled her fly rod and slipped on the reel. "That's an interesting reel," he said. "Don't think I've seen one of those before. That isn't a Bogdan trout reel by chance?"

"It is," said Lew with a proud grin. "Gift from my friend, here." She yanked a thumb toward Osborne.

"Doc?" Bruce looked astonished. "Those can cost two thousand bucks or more!"

"I found it at an estate sale of an old friend of mine who collected fly rods and reels," said Osborne. "Didn't pay that much." He didn't disclose that he had paid $500: a cheap price to pay for the wonder on Lew's face when she had unwrapped her birthday gift.

"May I see?" asked Bruce. Lew handed over her fly rod and Bruce ran admiring eyes over the reel. "I hear they only make a hundred of these a year. Is it worth the money?"

"It is in my book," said Lew. "You pay for the engineering—the drag is exquisite. Smooth, strong. Since I've been using this reel, I've never had my fly line break. I don't know that I catch more fish with this reel but I sure as heck land more."

"Can I try it later?" asked Bruce.

"Sure."

"So, Chief, you nymph fishing today?" Bruce turned a critical eye on the water. "I don't see a hatch of any kind."

"Dry flies for me," said Lew, patting the box of trout flies she had tucked into her shirt pocket.

"Oh, really. What do you see?"

"Nothing, Bruce. I just like dry fly fishing—it's prettier."

"That's not very scientific," said Bruce, taken aback.

"No, it's not," said Lew with a shrug. "But it's what I feel like today."

While they spoke, Osborne had been perusing the water. The river was narrow near the landing with a slight current: more placid than he had been expecting, which was a relief. He knew this river was popular among kayakers but he wasn't familiar with it.

Osborne rarely fished rivers. Their depths varied too much, and he detested the dead timbers submerged since the logging era and lurking just deep enough to sabotage the prop on your outboard. Rivers gave him the creeps.

"Ready, everyone? Man your boats." Ray's excitement was so infectious even Lew slipped into her kayak with enthusiasm, the worry that had been badgering her over the last few days gone for the moment.

"Doc? Need a hand?" Ray waded into the water to hold Osborne's kayak steady as he got seated. "Everyone, listen up—I got your fishing rods right where you can reach 'em easy."

"How far do we go before we stop to cast a few?" asked Lew.

"Not sure. I haven't been here before," said Ray. "A buddy told me about this river—said it's got northern pike, steelhead trout—nice big fish. I figure we go down twenty minutes or so and see where we're at. Sound good?"

Nothing about it sounded good to Osborne: What if he hooked a huge northern? How the hell do you land a fish that big from a one-man kayak that puts you nose to nose with a rack of evil teeth? He threw a questioning look at Lew but she was busy using her paddle to push away from the shoreline.

"Whoopee!" shouted Bruce as he shoved off.

Lew and Osborne followed with Ray bringing up the rear.

The August morning was lovely, warm and clear. As the kayaks moved soundlessly with the current, Osborne began to rethink his prejudice against rivers: *Oh, man, this silence is music.* An eagle circled overhead and a kingfisher darted from bush to bush. A Great Blue Heron launched from the riverbank with a swoop of its magnificent wings.

As Lew glided by, she said, "Hard to find fault with the world on a day like this."

"I knew you'd like it, kiddo," said Osborne. "Aren't you happy I twisted your arm?" She smiled and nodded.

They rounded a bend and heard a soft rumbling in the distance. The sound grew louder and Osborne wondered if they were hearing a sawmill or some other machinery used by loggers.

Even as he speculated, he felt the current grab the kayak, pulling it faster, faster. Twenty yards in front of him, he saw the bow of Lew's kayak go up, up, and up. Suddenly she was over and out of the boat. Before he could register that they had hit rapids, his kayak was tipped sideways and out he flew into the river.

The water could not have been more than a foot and a half deep, but the bottom was rocky and the current pounding. Osborne grabbed for the back end of his kayak, trying to keep his shoulders and head out of the water. His legs were useless as the current battered them against the rocks. Fear rose: was he going to break his legs?

Lew was still ahead of him, clutching her kayak and, somehow, managing to drift off to the left toward the riverbank. Osborne knew if he could get there, too, he could at least get his feet under him. Fighting to see, he got his head above the frothing water long enough to see Ray looking down from his kayak with worry as he was swept by, "Are you okay, Doc?"

"How the hell should I know?" said Osborne, adding a string of words that he rarely used but that fit the occasion. As he cleared the rapids, he was able to kick and paddle off toward the shoreline just beyond where Lew had managed to get her footing.

"Oh, no, Doc—grab my rod," she cried as her fly rod floated by him. A sweatshirt followed, but Osborne opted to scramble for the fly rod. As he did so, his glasses case went floating by. By some stroke of luck, he was able to grab that, too.

Crawling on his hands and knees, Osborne managed to get out of the water, hauling his kayak behind him. He threw himself on the sand near Lew who was sitting, knees akimbo, breathing hard. "I am so bruised," she said, "I'll bet you my legs will be purple tonight."

"I'm glad we're alive," said Osborne. "You can drown out there."

"Tell me," said Lew. "Ray should have told us about the rapids. Hey, here comes the guilty party."

"You two did everything all wrong," said Ray walking up river and pulling his kayak behind him. "When you fall out of a boat like that, don't fight the rapids. Rely on your life vest and float feet out in front—use your feet to push off the rocks."

"Use your head and shut up," said Osborne. "You almost killed us. Why didn't you tell us about the rapids?"

"Ray Pradt, I bet you anything those are Class Four rapids," said Lew. "Are you out of your mind?"

"I didn't know. Believe me, I didn't know."

Ray was so stricken, Osborne took a deep breath and did his best to calm down.

"Do we have any idea where we are?" asked Lew. "My cell phone drowned. Can't use that to call for help."

"Ray, I think we've had our excitement. I'm ready to call it a day," said Osborne.

"Me, too," said Lew. "I need bandages." She offered up her left leg with a scrape along the shin.

Ray heaved his kayak onto the shore, reached into it for a small hand pump, and started to pump the water from Osborne's kayak.

"If I can get us all going again, I know that George Stocker's got a place on the river. Down a ways still but we can beach there, borrow a vehicle, and I'll go get the truck so we can load up the kayaks. Or did you want to fish?"

The glares from Osborne and Lew answered his question.

"I'm soaked and I'm cold and I want dry clothes," said Lew. "Where's Bruce?"

"Oh, he's okay. After we saw you two go over, we hugged the far right side of the falls and made it fine. He's waiting for us down around the bend."

"Not fair," said Lew.

When Ray had got enough water pumped from each kayak so that they could tip the rest out, Osborne and Lew were able to climb back into their boats. When they reached Bruce, they found he had managed to grab Lew's sweatshirt as it floated by: all was not lost.

Chapter Twenty-Eight

"For the third time, I demand to see my child," said Gladys Daniels, grinding out her words.

"Mrs. Daniels, I really, really don't think that is a good idea," said the director of the funeral parlor. "Your daughter's remains have been prepared with care for the crematorium. To view the departed now would only cause you more emotional distress. Please, let me help you plan the memorial—"

"Damn you, I insist," said Gladys, pounding her fist on his desk. "Let me be clear, young man, I am not leaving this building until I have seen my daughter." Her voice rose in near hysteria.

"All right, all right." The funeral director raised his hands in surrender. "I'll alert the staff."

Gladys drove straight home, marched into the big house and straight into the dining room, where she pulled open the top drawer in the dining room buffet. She reached under the linen place mats for the gun case. She loaded the revolver and tucked it into her purse.

She would wait until dark. Just like that fat wife had waited in the shadows for Cynthia.

"Don't you try to tell me Cynthia had an 'accident' in the boathouse," Gladys muttered out loud. "I know exactly what happened. Jim must have called just like he used to and invited her for an evening on his boat."

A sad smile crossed Gladys's face as she recalled how happy Cynthia had been after the first time she had spent an evening with Jim McNeil on his boat. That was what had been so special between Gladys and Cynthia: mother and child told each other everything.

When it came to Jim McNeil, Cynthia shared every detail. That's when Gladys knew deep in her heart that those two were meant for each other. You don't have a love affair as intense as theirs and not be meant to spend your lives together.

That slimy little Jennifer had hit on him, clouding his judgment—as it would any healthy male. But not for long. Gladys had seen to that.

Flashing the money had made it easy for her to convince young Alvin to take care of the little bitch. Maybe it was the drugs he was taking, but he was none too bright, that dummy. Now, with him long gone, who would ever know?

And just as she had taken care of Alvin, she would see to the fat wife, too. *My child is dead and it is all her fault, all her fault, all her fault. . . .*

All she had to do now was get the bitch out of her house.

Chapter Twenty-Nine

Doc and Lew scrambled up the riverbank behind Ray and Bruce, grabbing tag alder branches for support. At the crest of the steep bank, they found themselves staring down into a ravine someone was using as a dump. Discarded appliances, old doors, paint cans, bedsprings, broken-down farm equipment, rusted-out cars, and rolls of discarded chicken wire littered the pit below.

"Where on earth are we?" asked Lew. "Whew! This place smells of dead animals."

"This is ol' George Stocker's place," said Ray. "He cuts wood, hauls trash—whatever you'll pay him for."

"He hauls trash, all right," said Lew. "He's in violation of county regs on this crap. Look, there's a refrigerator with the door still on." Lew pointed to a large, white upright appliance that had been dumped on its side near the edge of the pit. "That's against the law. Some little kid could crawl in and die."

"Chief," said Ray, "can we go easy on old George? He can't afford fines. Old man has a hard enough time making ends meet to buy food. C'mon, let's see if he's home and has a vehicle I can borrow."

The four of them picked their way along the edge of the ravine. Beyond the pit was a sandy, weedy trail, which wound around a small bog green with algae and along two rows of stacked firewood.

On the other side of the firewood, Osborne saw a patchwork hovel of boards and windows: someone's excuse for living quarters. An ancient Ford pickup was parked near a dilapidated shed whose roof had caved in. A beat-up van that had once belonged to a plumber, his name painted over with a couple swipes of white paint, was parked in front of the house.

Knocking at the front door, Ray hollered, "George? You home, you razzbonya?"

Yes, George was home. "Ray Pradt? What the hell? What brings you to this neck of the woods?"

The man who opened the door had a face like Santa Claus: round and sunburn red with bleary eyes visible above a dirty gray beard that ballooned onto his chest. Filthy overalls over a T-shirt with its sleeves ripped off completed the picture. Osborne figured George Stocker weighed in the neighborhood of three hundred pounds and would have found a teeth cleaning to be a terrifying experience.

"My friends and I had a problem on those river rapids back a ways," said Ray. He gestured toward Lew and Osborne who were so wet their clothes clung to them. "I need to get them back to their vehicles parked up at the public landing. Got time to give me a ride?"

"Yep, I can do that," said George, hawking a wad of tobacco off to one side. "Got a little something to cover my gas?"

"Five bucks do it?" asked Ray.

"Umm, you betcha."

"Mr. Stocker," said Lew, stepping forward, "I'm Chief Ferris with the Loon Lake Police Department and I don't like what I see on your back forty there. Looks to me like you got some toxic chemicals back there. You got a permit for all that dumping?"

The look George gave her answered that question. "Nope. Never needed one. Been hauling for folks 'round here for years. Ain't nobody said nothin' to me never."

"Maybe so, but the county maintains a landfill for that specific purpose—and you are dumping too close to the river to boot."

"Landfill costs money. Some folks can't pay." He spat again. Osborne worried Ray's ride was about to disappear. They were at least ten miles from where they had put in. He put an arm across

Lew's shoulders and whispered, "Take it easy." She shrugged his arm off.

"Mr. Stocker, are you married?" Lew asked.

"Yep, but my wife passed last year."

"Do you have grandchildren?"

"Yep. Got six of 'em."

"Do they visit you here?"

"Sure. Most weekends, why? I watch 'em times my daughter works at Wal-Mart."

"I'll make you a deal," said Lew. "If you will take the door off that refrigerator you got sitting on the edge of the dump, I'll not bug you about the rest of the trash right away. I'll give you a year to get the hazards cleaned up."

"Great idea," said Ray, "George, I'll help. I got a buddy with a backhoe. Hell, we'll just bury everything."

"Hold on, Ray," said Lew. "Talk to me before you do that."

"Absolutely," said Ray. "Me and George—we'll do up a plan. Sound good to you, George?"

George appeared to give a rat's ass. "C'mon, Pradt," he said, "I'll give you a lift in my van. The rest of you wanna pile in the back?"

"No thanks, we'll wait here," said Osborne. "Ray, why don't you get my car? Keys are behind the rear license plate. That way we can all drive back, then you and Bruce come back here for the kayaks. Does that work?"

"Wait a minute," said Lew. "George, you got tools close by? While you and Ray get the car, we'll take care of getting the door off that appliance down there."

George shrugged and said, "Ain't a refrigerator, it's a freezer. Tools in the back of my truck over there. You might wanna take a hammer or somethin'—the old lady padlocked the damn thing. Don't hurt yourselves."

After they drove off, Lew turned to Bruce and Osborne. "Give me a hand with that freezer. You know damn well that once we leave here, the old man won't take care of it. Knowing he has little kids running around this place—I'll have nightmares if we leave that door on."

Two blows of the hammer and Bruce had the padlock popped off the freezer door. What remained of Alvin Marski greeted them with a blast of bad air. The combination of an unplugged freezer and the hot August sun had done its damage. Only the blue jeans and the blue Oxford shirt were identifiable. Even Bruce had to back off, way off.

On the shelf above Alvin was a plastic bag holding a decomposing critter nestled in red fur. The bag was labeled "P. Osborne" in black marker. It was the fox that Osborne had given to Marv Daniels for mounting shortly before Marv's death years ago.

"Too bad Dr. Cynthia Daniels isn't around to answer a few questions," said Lew later that afternoon. Bruce had stayed with the freezer and the body while she and Osborne had raced to town to change clothes, then hurried back to the site just as an ambulance arrived for the body along with a tow truck that could move the freezer.

"I would like to know how and why Alvin Marski ended up in her mother's freezer," said Lew.

"If I remember right," said Osborne, "that's the freezer Marv used for his taxidermy business. He used it to store carcasses until he had time to work on them. I remember him telling me how hard it was to find one large enough to hold a bear."

"Or a man," said Lew. "Bruce did an initial exam at the morgue and he is quite sure Alvin took at least one bullet in the head—maybe more. And there appear to be bullets lodged in the interior walls of the freezer. He sent the corpse down to Wausau for a complete autopsy.

"He found bloodstains on the shoes that he said don't match the blood patterning from the bullet wounds so he's going to have those tested, too. Thank goodness, poor Alvin had a wallet on him—could have taken months to identify those remains otherwise."

"Lew, the boy only had a few dollars in that wallet. Why would someone kill a guy for a few bucks?"

A knock at the door to Lew's office and Dani poked her head in. "Can I interrupt? Chief Ferris, I got something here you have got to see. Really, I need to show you right away."

"Will it take long?"

"No, just a few minutes. But look at this," said Dani setting her laptop computer on Lew's desk and motioning for Lew and Osborne to gather behind her in order to see what she had on the screen.

"This is my Facebook page, and remember I told you Chet Junior 'friended' me right away? Well, you won't believe what he posted for everyone to see. . . .

"There—that tattoo?" Dani clicked on a lurid tattoo that read "The Enforcer."

"That's his profile picture. Then he posted this."

Dani stepped back so Lew and Osborne could read the sentences next to the profile tattoo: *Just got off the phone with my dad. He's hiring me to be the new Chief of the Loon Lake Police Department. I'm packing my guns, guys and gals. Can't wait to get up there and kick some ass.*"

"Whoa," said Lew. "That is highly inappropriate language for a law enforcement professional."

"Unbelievable," said Dani. "Now you know why I've been bugging you."

"I think we have an excellent case against hiring this guy," said Osborne. "Why don't you let me take care of the discussion with his father, Lewellyn?"

"This could ruin that kid's career," said Lew. "What a shame."

"A shame maybe," said Osborne, "but that kid sounds like a real razzbonya. Worse than his old man."

Two days later, Dani and Osborne met with Chet Tillman in his office at City Hall.

"What's up, Doc?" asked Chet with a chuckle at his little joke. Osborne gave a polite smile in response.

"Chet, we have a problem," said Osborne. "I understand that you and the town council have decided to bring your son in as a replacement for Chief Lewellyn Ferris. Is that correct?"

"You betcha," said Chet, rocking back in his swivel chair and crossing his hands on his wide belly. "Yep, got Chet Junior starting day after New Year's. We need young blood in the department."

Osborne turned to Dani: "Would you download the Facebook file that Chet Junior posted, please?" Dani opened her laptop, hit a few keys, and waited. Meanwhile, Chet rocked back and forth in his chair while gazing out the window.

"Grouse hunting this fall, Doc?" he asked as the minutes passed.

"Ready," said Dani. Osborne reached for the laptop, walked around the desk to stand next to Chet, and leaned over to show him his son's Facebook profile and the ugly posting.

Chet stared. "So? I don't see what the problem is."

Leaving the laptop in front of the man, Osborne returned to his chair. "I didn't think you would, Chet. So I ran it by Leo and Burt," he said, referring to the county sheriff and his chief deputy. "They find your son's language highly inappropriate for a law enforcement officer. They also said that numerous law enforcement agencies have fired officers in similar circumstances."

"*Fired?*" Chet sat up straight, his face turning bright pink. "What the hell—*fired?*"

"Fired," said Osborne in a quiet, deliberate tone.

"And you showed this to the sheriff's department?" The incredulity in Chet's voice made Osborne wish Lew was there to hear the conversation.

"I thought a professional opinion was in order." Osborne knew he sounded like he was recommending twenty thousand dollars worth of dental implants.

"Hmm," Chet swiveled his chair around to stare at the wall behind him. "Hmm."

"Leo had a suggestion, Chet. Would you like to hear it?"

Chet made an attempt to brush back the hair that had disappeared from his forehead long ago. With a pained expression on his face, he said, "All right—what did Leo say?"

"He suggested you leave Lewellyn Ferris in her position for the time being and arrange for Chet Junior to join the sheriff's department as a deputy in training. If he does well and understands the needs of the county and the town, then he will be promotable."

"But he's already put in five years on the force in St. Paul. You're asking him to repeat that?"

"It may not be five years. If you and your son will agree to this arrangement and if that young man can prove that he has matured in his attitude toward the public whom he is expected to serve (Osborne left out the words he wanted to use: *serve not bully*) then he may have a successful career in law enforcement in this region."

"I'll take care of it," said Chet. He pointed to the Facebook page on the laptop: "This stays confidential?"

"If your son will take it down it does."

"Agreed. I'll let him know he'll be reporting to Leo."

"Good," said Osborne. "He should contact Leo's assistant right away. There's paperwork to be completed, tests to take—the usual." He got to his feet as Dani scooped up and closed the laptop.

"One more thing, Chet," said Osborne as he reached the door, "I'll have Chief Ferris tear up those retirement papers."

Chet nodded.

Two hours later, Chet Junior disappeared from Facebook.

Chapter Thirty

Late that evening Leigh settled onto the family room sofa to watch an *American Idol* episode she had taped two weeks ago. Hard to believe how life had changed in such a short time. She couldn't get over how relaxed she felt. Even with Jim moved out, she was comfortable. His absence was hardly new, but how she felt about it was different.

The afternoon session with her therapist had helped. For one thing, deciding the friendly intimacy of their early years together was to be treasured, not resented, made her feel less duped. *People change*, she thought, pouring herself a glass of wine. *People change and you can't stop that from happening.*

She realized now what she had refused to admit for so long: Jim desired other women. Maybe he always would. Did he substitute sex for intimacy? Maybe.

She didn't. Friendship and closeness meant so much to her. And she was just forty—not too old to start over.

Leigh's heart warmed at the thought of Ray Pradt. The relationship book she was reading talked about "transition people": the people who attract you in the early months after you've ended a long-term relationship—they help restore your self-esteem. Could Ray be her "transition person"? Sure he was younger than she was, but so much fun! And so cute!

The sound of a car pulling up in the drive surprised her. Must be Jim back for one more suitcase. She got to her feet and peeked through the living room curtains. The sedan out front was not Jim's car, nor the police cruiser that had been parked for hours in the drive. As she watched, a short, dark figure got out and walked toward the front door.

After one peal of the doorbell, Leigh opened the door. An elderly woman stood there. In spite of the warm, humid evening, she wore a purple trench coat, buttoned and belted. Leigh had never seen her before.

Her face was deathly white under flat black curls that appeared glued to her forehead. A slash of too-red lipstick emphasized the puckering around her lips. Intense black eyes searched Leigh's face as she said, "I am so sorry to drop in like this, but I have a . . . a terrible favor to ask." The woman choked, coughed once, and pressed a Kleenex to her eyes.

Leigh got the sense she was about to break down. "Cynthia Daniels was my daughter and I was hoping—I know this is a great deal to ask. . . ."

"Oh golly, I am so sorry," said Leigh with a surge of sympathy mixed with alarm. This was going to be difficult. "I'll try to help, but I didn't really know your daughter."

As she spoke she wondered if this woman knew of her daughter's obsession with Jim and her stalking of their home. She doubted it.

So far, while deciding whether or not to fire Jim, the clinic board had managed to keep a lid on that information. No one wanted the clinic to be tainted by full disclosure of the bizarre behavior of one of their esteemed physicians. "It will make our entire operation look schizophrenic—like we're incapable of hiring stable people," Jim had reported to Leigh.

"I would like to see where my daughter died. Just that. It will help me deal with my loss." She shook her head and a tear escaped one eye. "Would you have a moment to show me? I'll only take a moment. . . ."

"Of course," said Leigh, "if it helps you reach some sense of closure, I can do that. If you'll wait one minute, I'll get a flashlight and we'll walk down to the boathouse."

The woman dabbed at her eyes and blew her nose. "Thank you," she whispered. "I'll wait here."

Leigh hurried into the kitchen and grabbed a flashlight from the utility drawer. Her purse lay on the counter. Leigh hesitated, then reached into her purse for the small handgun. She slipped it out of its holster and into the pocket of her sweat pants. Just to be safe.

Could be raccoons out tonight. Besides, something about the old woman arriving in the dark. . . . She felt bad thinking that way but she also did not feel safe.

"All set," she said lightly, stepping through the front door. "Follow me and watch where you walk."

The solar lanterns that Jim had had installed earlier that summer emitted a soft glow along the sloping path leading to the boathouse. As they approached, Leigh turned to see if the older woman was having any difficulty with the stairs leading onto the outer deck. Light from the moon overhead caught a gleam of metal in the old woman's hand.

Leigh entered a dream. She saw fire spit from the barrel. She felt the handgun in her own hand as she fired. She woke in the emergency room with her husband sitting beside her.

"Jim? Am I alive?"

"Very much so, sweetheart. You've been out cold for over an hour." He placed a cool washcloth on her forehead. "The neighbors heard gunshots and called nine-one-one. You are very lucky. The bullet from Mrs. Daniels's gun grazed your skull. You'll have a scar and a headache but you'll survive."

"Oh . . ." Leigh reached up to feel the bandage on the side of her head. "A lot of blood?"

"Don't worry about that. If you're feeling better, Chief Ferris needs to speak with you."

Leigh pushed herself up on the pillow and reached for the glass of water beside the bed. "I'm a little shaky but I'm okay. What happened to—?"

"Your bullet hit an artery. She bled out before anyone could get there."

"Jim," said Leigh, tears pushing against her eyelids, "I want to sell the house. That boathouse. . . ."

"I know." Jim patted her hand.

Chapter Thirty-One

Osborne gazed out across the pond that fronted Lew's property. Saucers of palest rose, lavender, and mauve hovered overhead as they sat in the wooden swing, swaying gently back and forth.

Fresh corn from her garden, a pan-fried batch of bluegills that she had caught with the fly rod off her dock that morning, and a lemon meringue pie that Osborne had tried his hand on—with moderate success—had made for a delicious late summer meal.

"Ray has been teaching Leigh how to fish for muskie," said Osborne as he sipped his cup of coffee. "She wants to learn to fly fish and asked me to see if you might have time for a lesson or two?"

Lew leaned back, letting the light breezes off the water flow over her. Osborne enjoyed seeing her so relaxed. The retirement issue had been put away for the time being, erasing the worried look in her eyes.

Yes, Chet Tillman Junior would be working in the sheriff's department, but Leo had assured Osborne that, given the Facebook misstep, the young deputy's chances for advancement would be limited. At least, that was Leo's opinion at this time. "He has a lot to prove," the sheriff had said in a meeting with Lew, "a lot to prove."

"I'll be happy to get Leigh started with casting technique," said Lew. "But I've got quite a schedule these days. She would be better off joining Trout Unlimited and attending some of their workshops. Think she's serious about Ray? That could be a mistake."

"Not sure," said Osborne. "He told me they've talked things over—neither one of them wants a serious commitment."

"We've heard that before," said Lew with a chuckle. "The ladies always think they can change his mind."

"Speaking of workshops, how is your online course going?" asked Osborne. Once the retirement issue was no longer a concern, Lew had enrolled in a graduate course on criminal psychology.

"Very interesting," said Lew. "I'm studying personality disorders."

"With Gladys Daniels as a case study?" asked Osborne. Lew gave him the dim eye. "Just kidding."

"She fits the profile of someone living in their own weird reality, that's for sure," said Lew.

"She believed her own lies," said Osborne. "For years."

"She was canny," said Lew. "If Bruce hadn't found that envelope in the pickup that Alvin borrowed, if the blood splatters on Alvin's shoes hadn't matched Jennifer's DNA—we may not have linked her to the killing of Jennifer Williams, but when the DNA analysis on the saliva matched hers, we had a connection."

"I felt bad pressing his mother for information," said Osborne. "She was able to tell us that Alvin did odd jobs for Gladys. That explains how they knew each other."

"Even then I might not have had a case," said Lew. "But with two of the bullets from her gun lodged in Alvin's skull—the Wausau boys were able to match the bullets to that Smith & Wesson revolver of hers—"

"We'll never know for sure," said Osborne. "But I could swear that the knife Alvin used on Jennifer was one of Marv's taxidermy tools."

"Enough shop talk, Doc. Let's enjoy the evening."

They rocked back and forth. The lily pads were taking on a golden hue in the lowering sun; the rhythm of the swing matched the ripples on the pond. Sometimes an evening can punctuate your life with loveliness. It was that kind of evening.